2007 Contents

p55

p134

J. Campbell Kerr Paintings

p63

JIM shivered and pulled his jacket closer around him. What a way to spend the last few minutes of the year — stuck on a freezing doorstep with a lump of coal, a tin of shortbread and a bottle of whisky. It mightn't have been so bad if he could have had a wee dram, but his sister, Meg, had warned him against opening either tin or bottle until he was safely back in the house after the magic hour of midnight.

"It's just like when we were bairns," she said. "Only then it was Mam sending you out to make sure that our first visitor of the New Year would be dark and male."

"Yes, and poor old you, being fair and female, had to stay put by a roaring coal fire!" he mocked.

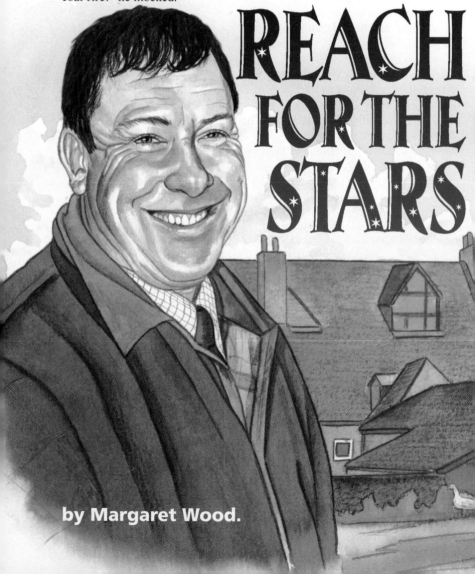

REACH FOR THE STARS

by Margaret Wood.

£6.25

Dear Reader,

WHAT a wonderful treat we have in store for you this year in the "Friend" Annual 2007. The year is going to get off to a flying start with 23 brand-new stories from all of your favourite authors.

If you're in the mood for a trip down memory lane, a wry smile or just a good old-fashioned read, we've got everything you could ever want here.

We also take our usual trip round the beauty that is Britain with the lovely paintings of J. Campbell Kerr, and look back fondly on the women who made music through the dark days of WWII and brought a little light into our lives.

Kathleen O'Farrell takes us on a poetic journey, too, as she charts the romance and wedding day of the couple on our cover.

There really is something for everyone in this year's Annual, so why not sit back and enjoy yourself? Remember that if you like what you see, you can always buy your "People's Friend" every week in your local newsagent's!

The Editor

Complete Stories

p142

The Wedding

Wartime Chanteuses & Entertainers

At that, Meg gave him a light tap with a handy newspaper and, for a moment, it was as if they were children again, instead of a pair of respectable pensioners.

"Anyway," he said, running a hand over hair which was still dark, but rapidly thinning, "I don't know if I've enough of this left to make me eligible as a first foot."

"Well, you're the best we've got," she said briskly. "So just get on with it."

Quarter to twelve seemed far too early to be pushed on to the doorstep, but Meg insisted that she was taking no chances with the clocks being wrong. It was hard enough to find good luck these days without tempting Providence. And though Jim might have insisted that his watch had never yet let him down, he held his tongue. He had a lot to thank his big sister for, not least for the way she had helped him through the last eighteen months since Eileen died.

HE set the New Year gifts down on the doorstep and blew on his hands. If Meg hadn't been in such a hurry to get him out he might have remembered to take his gloves. Mum had always made sure he put them on, along with his knitted balaclava.

But at least there was one consolation — nowadays he wasn't scared of the dark. It had taken him a long time to outgrow that childish fear, and it was Eileen who had finally cured him — one New Year's Eve, oddly enough.

"Look at the sky," she'd said. "It's like black velvet scattered with diamonds. Don't you just love it?"

They had been standing on this very doorstep. They'd been no more than bairns really, still at school. But even then he knew that she was special, and he found himself agreeing.

That night he had promised her the stars, and when he placed the tiny diamond on her finger only a few years later she had called it "her first star".

In the last days of her illness he had tried to tell her how sorry he was for failing to keep that promise. She had pressed a finger to his lips to silence him.

"You gave me two wonderful stars," she said.

At first he didn't know what she meant.

"Colin and Shona, silly. I didn't make them all on my own, you know!" For a moment the twinkle which her illness had dimmed was back in her eye.

Eileen had been right. Their children *were* stars. Colin had proved that over and over again after his mother passed on. And Shona, wee Shona, well, she had given him three wonderful grandchildren. He'd had a video from them at Christmas time with a tour of their beautiful new home and garden in Sydney.

Illustration by
Sally Rowe.

7

At the end, they had all gathered to give him a message.

"Come and visit us soon, Grandpops!" they'd chorused.

If only they knew how much he had wanted to say "yes". But the thought of being trapped in a metal box, thousands of feet up and suspended by goodness knew what, filled him with complete dread. He could have done it with Eileen by his side, but on his own . . .

✳   ✳   ✳   ✳

Jim looked at his watch. Surely it must nearly be midnight? His toes were frozen from standing still. He stamped down the garden path, past the big bush where ghosts and ghouls had lurked in his childish imagination. Surely if he could conquer one fear, he could deal with another?

He looked up at the inky sky awash with diamonds and suddenly, he could imagine Eileen's voice, as clear, as though she were standing beside him.

"If you offer someone the stars, Jim Sinclair, you've got to be prepared to go up there and get them . . ."

He gave a little chuckle. Eileen had always been the practical one. And this wasn't the first wee lecture she'd given him since she'd passed on. She was often popping into his head to remind him about eating proper meals or putting on a clean shirt. It was what kept him going.

Then it suddenly occurred to him that if he did make the long trip to the other side of the world, he wouldn't be going on his own. In a way, Eileen would always be with him.

ACROSS the frosty air came the bells of the town hall clock. It was New Year and a time for resolutions. Jim had already made his. He would go to Australia. He wouldn't let a little thing like fear of flying keep him from his "stars".

As soon as he rang the bell Meg opened the door, the traditional greeting on her lips. Then she relieved him of his gifts and pushed him towards the sitting-room.

"Away and sit beside the fire," she said. "You must be frozen."

"Well, if you hadn't shoved me out so early . . ."

The words hung on Jim's lips. Meg's cosy sitting-room was full of people — people whom he had last seen on his own television screen. He could hardly believe it!

"Shona. But how . . . ?" It was all he could manage to get out past the lump in his throat and the ball of happiness forming in his chest.

His daughter came towards him, smiling broadly.

"Back door," she said, and her arms went round him in a hug. "Happy New Year, Dad. We've come for your answer."

Jim knew immediately what she meant.

"It's yes, lass. It's yes. And a very happy New Year to you, too." ■

À La Mode

SOME say the name is rather grand — Fiona's
   Fashion Wear —
When really it's a draper's, on a corner of the square.
But though it's small, Fiona's shop is popular all round
And enjoys a reputation that is very, very sound.

For when it comes to needlework, as everybody knows,
Miss Fiona puts her heart in everything she sews.
There's magic in her fingertips, and into every seam,
With every tiny little stitch, she weaves a lovely dream.

"Now, Jeanie, dear, stand still,"
   she says (she's known Jean
   all her days),
And Jean, upon the little stool,
   so readily obeys,
For, when she wears this lovely
   dress her joy will be
   complete,
And, thanks to Miss Fiona's
   flair, it's coming on a treat.

Hamish will be so proud
   of her, she thinks, with
   happy smile,
When, gracefully, on
   Father's arm, she floats
   along the aisle.
For it will thrill him
   through and through,
   and fill him with delight,
To see her come towards him,
   her lovely face alight,
with such deep joy and
   happiness —
   and he'll love her
even more —
   Looking twice as pretty
      as she's ever
         looked before!
— Kathleen O'Farrell.

JOCK LAMBERT had brought in his sister Hetty to care for his infant daughter, Rosie, after his wife died. He'd felt a pang of misgiving as Hetty had turned up, carrying her belongings in a borrowed suitcase. Her ration book and the treasured pictures of her favourite film stars were safely tucked away in the crocheted shoulder bag she always carried with her, along with stumps of lipsticks and an almost empty phial of Phul-Nana perfume.

Aged seventeen, Hetty looked liked a child herself, and an intractable one at that. Small and defiant, she had a mop of unruly brown hair and what he thought looked suspiciously like rouge on her cheeks. This was a less than satisfactory arrangement, Hetty being on the flighty side and always wanting to be out dancing and going to the pictures and suchlike with her friends. But it was a risk Jock had to take, since he had no other female relatives able and willing to take on the job of bringing up his daughter.

Hetty had been spoiled, that was the problem, what with being the only girl and so much younger than the rest of them. She would have to curb some of her daft ways if she was to settle down and manage the household without an older woman to advise her.

Jock had reckoned without Hetty's defiant streak, however, which had caused her to defy him.

"I love Rosie like she was mine, Jock, but I do need some life of my own as well! Surely you don't begrudge me the occasional night off? Anyway, it's about time you spent some evenings with your daughter. She hardly knows who you are!"

And at the sight of the baby's unblinking eyes, so like his wife's, Jock had busied himself with making up the fire. He wasn't a man given to open emotion.

A Promise Is A Promise

by Marie West.

"Don't be back late," he'd call after Hetty, knowing even as he said it that he might as well talk to the wall. She could be so exasperating, determinedly heading off on an evening out with her friend, Edith, before returning home flushed and happy, and chattering fifty to the dozen.

Hetty just wasn't like other women, that was the top and bottom of it. She could drive you to distraction at times! Still, as time went on, Jock had to admit that his daughter was being well cared for and was turning out to be a credit to them. Her mother would have been proud of her.

Rosie, for her part, adored Aunt Hetty, who smelled magically of vanishing cream and French Moss talcum powder and the occasional lingering scent of the perfume she'd dab behind her ears when she went out with her friends.

Hetty had shown Rosie photographs of a pretty woman with long dark hair.

"That's your mam, Rosie. She had big blue eyes, just like you."

She rummaged among the

Illustration by
Shane Marsh.

photographs. "And that's your mam and dad on their wedding day."

Rosie often complained that she wasn't bonnie like her mother or Hetty, or even Dorothy, who was her best friend at school.

"Of course you're bonnie, pet! Don't let anyone ever tell you different," Aunt Hetty had insisted. "Just you wait and see. You'll be the image of your mam when you grow up — there'll be no-one to touch you. Meantime, let's do something about your hair."

Rosie would sit patiently while Hetty laboriously wound her straight hair into rags, which would be combed out into ringlets the next day and tied up with bright ribbons so that Rosie would feel as bonnie as Dorothy, who had blonde curls and always managed to keep her white socks clean.

It was Dorothy who had boasted to Rosie about her own Aunt Susannah, who was going to be married in the Methodist church, where they went to Sunday school, and who had said that Dorothy could be a bridesmaid in a pink satin dress. Rosie, who hadn't realised that aunts could get married, had gone to Aunt Hetty when she got home.

"Are you going to get married, Aunt Hetty?"

"Why no, of course not," had been the reply. "I'd rather stay here and look after you and your dad. Why would I want to get married and leave you?" And Hetty had brushed away the memory of the summer when she was seventeen, just before Jock had lost his young wife and had been in need of her help.

The memory of eighteen-year-old Thomas, who'd worked at Dollin's High Class Provisions, but who had been leaving soon for his National Service, lingered still. Thomas had fastened daisies in her hair and kissed her one evening, as they'd walked home along the promenade. He'd asked her to write to him while he was away, and she had been dizzy with happiness.

Then Connie had died, and she'd had to put Thomas out of her mind.

"If you did get married —" Rosie was insistent "— could I be your bridesmaid and wear a pink dress?"

"Of course. And a little coronet of roses in your hair."

Rosie was enchanted.

"Do you promise, Aunt Hetty? Cross your heart and hope to die?"

"Promise," Hetty had solemnly replied. "You have to promise as well, though. I don't want to be left without a chief bridesmaid!"

But Aunt Hetty never had married. Although Rosie was disappointed not to be a bridesmaid, she was relieved that Aunt Hetty wouldn't be leaving them. She wanted her aunt to stay with them for ever.

So Hetty had carried on looking after them, trying to do her best. If she sometimes thought wistfully of Thomas, and wondered where he was now, she was happy enough, and Rosie was flourishing under her care, which was what was important.

After all, life couldn't be all about soft summer evenings and flowers in your hair. When Jock tried to impose his own views on her too often, she would blithely go her own way, knowing that this was just his way, and that he'd never change.

OR so she believed. He'd eventually stopped arguing with her and trying to lay down the law. Afterwards, Hetty wondered if that was when she'd first realised that there was something really wrong with Jock. It was only after he'd had that spell in the infirmary that she'd found out how serious his illness was.

She'd brought him home as he was fretting so much in hospital. She'd had his bed moved to the window, from where he could watch all the comings and goings on his better days, and look out for Rosie returning from school.

"I went to see Rosie's teacher when you were in hospital, Jock. He thinks she's bound to pass the scholarship," Hetty said to him, as she brought him the bowl of soup which was all he seemed able to manage these days. "She's a clever girl, is our Rosie."

He'd turned to her — his sister, Henrietta, who had never grown into her name but had grown into someone he could depend on, even if she had always taken pleasure in defying him. He could recall the times when he'd been about to give her a piece of his mind, only to find her singing happily as she black-leaded the kitchen range, or dancing round the front room with a laughing Rosie in her arms. And then, somehow, he would stop being angry with her.

"Aye, well. You haven't made too bad a fist of things," he'd said gruffly.

Hetty was taken aback.

"You want to watch it, our Jock! You nearly said something nice about me!"

She'd managed to make it as far as the scullery before the threatened tears, kept in check for so long, had finally given way. She'd cried as if she would never stop.

When it was all over, and it seemed to Rosie that nothing would ever make her feel better, it had been Hetty who'd found the abandoned black and white kitten, half-dead from starvation, which needed Rosie's help to make it well again.

They'd placed the kitten in a box by the fire and fed it warm milk from a tiny doll's bottle until it was able to lap from a saucer. It had miraculously staggered about on its tiny feet, purring croakily in its unused voice, knowing somehow that it belonged not to Aunt Hetty, but to Rosie.

Remembering, the grown-up Rosie realised that this had been just one of the ways in which Hetty had done so much to try to help her cope with what had happened, even though she must have been unhappy herself.

The other thing that Rosie had never understood at the time was how desperately short of money they had been after her father died. His workmates in the shipyard had called round with a collection they'd made, which had helped, and then Hetty had found a job in the bakery which meant she could be home before Rosie came in from school.

They'd managed, somehow, but it couldn't have been easy.

It was only much later, looking back, that Rosie realised that Aunt Hetty had been little more than a girl herself when she'd first come to live with them — a young girl taking on the responsibility of running a household and bringing up her brother's child! It must have been a daunting task for someone so young.

From the distance which time had given, Rosie realised that her father, whom she'd loved dearly, had not been an easy man for Hetty to live with, being set in the ways of the time, even though there had been an unbreakable bond between brother and sister. She knew her father had loved Hetty in his own way.

As for herself, she knew that she had a debt to Aunt Hetty which she could never repay. It had been Hetty who, despite everything that had happened, had taught her how to be happy. And she *had* been happy. She had her beloved husband, Rob, and her children, who were now making their own way in life. She herself, if no longer exactly young, could look back with gratitude for the good times they had brought.

Today was to be another of those good times. Rosie thought that her most enduring memory of Aunt Hetty was of her working her way through a pile of ironing in the scullery, swaying along to the music of Edmundo Ros or whichever dance music happened to be playing on the wireless at that time. But there were other memories, too, and now, fifty years on, there was a promise she needed to keep.

HETTY had never lost touch with Edith, who had been widowed some time ago. It was one of those friendships which had been cemented in the days of their youth, and which was destined to last throughout their lives. The two women had grown old together, although Rosie would sometimes say that they were no different from the dizzy, laughing girls who had danced their way through their younger days.

It was the talk of such dancing which had aroused all those memories in Edith.

"Why don't we try one of those afternoon tea dances? It's bound to be full of older people, like ourselves, so we won't feel out of place. I'd love to hear some of that old music again," she'd added wistfully.

Hetty had agreed, remembering how, as young girls, they'd whirled round to the strains of "Begin The Beguine," and how captivated she'd been by the music.

So they'd found themselves in a dance hall once again, even if it was just the community centre, and it was as if they were back in the past, their feet remembering the steps as the music played. It was as they'd been sitting reminiscing that Hetty had been approached by a small, grey-haired man who'd seemed vaguely familiar.

He'd paused, unsure of himself.

"Hetty . . . Hetty Lambert? It is you! After all these years."

She'd known then.

The Palace of Holyroodhouse

LEGEND has it that King David I was hunting one day in 1128. His horse was startled by a stag which appeared from nowhere, and King David found himself hurled to the ground, in mortal danger of being gored by the stag's antlers. In desperation, he grasped hold of them, whereupon they miraculously changed into a Crucifix. That night, King David pledged to build an Abbey for Canons devoted to the Cross.

Holyrood means "Holy Cross".

Situated at the end of the Royal Mile, the Palace of Holyrood is the Queen's official residence in Scotland and the setting for State ceremonies and official entertaining.

J. CAMPBELL KERR.

"Well, Thomas, aren't you going to ask me to dance?"

They'd taken to the floor as though they'd been waiting to do so all their lives.

It had been the first of many meetings. They had so much to talk about, and so much catching up to do, that it seemed as if there wasn't enough time in the world for them.

It had been more than half a century since Thomas had kissed the young Hetty and threaded flowers in her hair, yet however much the years had changed them, their memories of one another hadn't dimmed.

As they'd talked, the years had rolled away, and it hadn't seemed to matter that they were maybe a little slower and stiffer than they'd been. What mattered was that they wanted to spend the rest of their lives together.

*   *   *   *

They had intended to slip away quietly to be married, but had been overruled by Rosie, who had, Hetty realised with some amusement, inherited some of her father's determined streak. Instead, there was to be a simple ceremony at the little church on the corner, and then they were to be whisked away to the big hotel where Rosie and Rob had arranged the reception. Rosie had made all the arrangements for the flowers and the catering and the music. She was wearing a pink silk dress, which she thought was probably much too young for her, but had drawn a line at a coronet in her hair. Instead, she was wearing a white rose on her hat.

At last, they were ready to leave. Hetty was wearing her favourite blue, but had been insistent, for some reason, that Rosie should fasten her hair up, with a daisy pinned at the back.

It was useless to point out to Hetty that it didn't match her dress. Capricious as ever, she wanted the daisy, so Rosie gave in with good grace. Her aunt was obviously still the same Hetty who had infuriated Rosie's father with her determination to have her way, and she wouldn't change now.

"How do I look?" Hetty asked, turning to face her.

"Really bonnie, pet," Rosie had replied. "There'll be no-one there to touch you."

It was a lovely wedding.

Edith, her eyes bright with tears, sighed as her friend stood with Thomas, both looking so happy.

"Mind, it took you long enough to get round to it. I've had that toaster wrapped up for nigh on a lifetime!"

Rosie went across to Hetty and her new husband.

"Come on, it's time for you two to start the dancing! I've requested your favourite music. I couldn't manage Joe Loss, but it's the next best thing."

As Hetty and Thomas glided off into their future together, to the beguiling music of the beguine, Rosie felt sure her father was looking down on them approvingly, pleased that his sister was finally finding the happiness she deserved, with the man that she loved. ■

by Lynne Hackles.

Illustration by Sally Rowe.

Shopping With Daniel

GRANNY, you've got black tickles round your eyes." Dan smiles at me, his missing front tooth making the grin even cheekier.

"Tickles?" I peer into the mirror, praying that this nit-picking five-year-old isn't pointing out my wrinkles to me. I don't need anyone to do that, not even my darling grandson.

"There," he says, kneeling on the bed where I've been sitting to apply my make-up. A little finger wipes away a smudge of mascara.

With a tissue in one hand and my magnifying mirror in the other I repair the damage and apply the final touch — lipstick.

17

Meanwhile, Dan leans against the headboard and pops the air pockets on the bubble-wrap bag in which I keep my magnifying mirror.

Make-up complete, I hand the mirror to him. This is a ritual we've been performing since he was old enough to sit up. Dan stares into the magnified side of the mirror.

"Big Dan," he announces.

Then he turns it round to the ordinary side.

"Little Dan."

Within seconds the chant begins as the mirror spins in his hands.

"Big Dan, Little Dan, Big Dan . . ."

"Can Big Dan go and put his shoes on while Granny gets changed?" I ask, retrieving the mirror and the bubble-free bubble-wrap.

He rolls carelessly off the bed and disappears in search of shoes. Quickly I pull on my new jeans and a bright red sweater.

"Why haven't I got a grandad?" he shouts from the bedroom he's claimed as his own when he stays over with me.

I pretend not to hear.

His head appears round the door.

"Seth's got one," he tells me. "Seth says grandads are cool. His plays footie with him and knows all about robots and he's going to take him to Robot Wars . . ."

IT'S the first time Dan has ever mentioned grandads, and his lack of one. Strange how the subject's never cropped up before.

Buckling my belt, I wonder how to explain divorce to a five-year-old.

"That's a cool belt," he says.

I look down at the belt, and then at him in surprise. The bright red belt has a silver buckle, and I remember buying it to go with a grey skirt I had when I was working at the building society, so that would make it at least twenty-five years old. At least twenty years older than Dan.

"Thanks." I begin to feel better about myself. An added bonus is that the subject has changed and grandads are no longer our topic of conversation.

Wrong!

"About grandads . . ." Those two little vertical frown lines have appeared at the top of his nose. "Where's mine?"

I pull him to me, wanting to haul him on to my lap as we sit on the bed. He struggles and ends up at my side. At five he's too old for sitting on laps.

"He's in Australia," I say. "He didn't want to stay here any longer so he went all the way to the other side of the world."

Dan tips his head to one side and his blue eyes stare into mine.

"Oh," he says. "So, when's he coming back?"

"He isn't." I stop myself before going into a long convoluted explanation.

"Never?"

I shake my head and leave Dan to digest these new facts, dreading what he'll come out with next. I can almost see his brain whirring.

"Well," he says, "could you get me another one?"

I shrug my shoulders, a gesture Dan copies. If only it was that easy. But fifty-something women aren't exactly spoiled for choice when it comes to finding new partners!

"It's not that easy . . ." I begin.

"I'll help you," Dan says.

My body breaks out in a cold sweat at the thought of it.

SETH'S granny has grey hair," Dan tells me as we lock the front door. Poor thing, I think, brushing my fingers through my dyed blonde fringe.

"But his grandad has black hair. I think he's a new one."

Not such a poor thing after all, eh? Sounds as if she's got herself a toy-boy!

"Shall I ask Seth where his gran got the new grandad from?"

My cold sweat from earlier turns into a hot flush.

"That might not be a very good idea."

"We'll just have to look for ourselves then," Dan says, climbing into the car.

"We could go to a grandad shop," I joke.

"Don't be silly." He folds his arms and stares straight ahead, deep in thought.

I change into my driving shoes, adjust my seat and lean across to search for my glasses in the glove-box. Catching sight of my reflection in the interior mirror, I tell myself I could pass for ten years younger. Well, perhaps on a good day.

I rub my specs on a tissue and slip them on. Dan comes out of his dream and stares wide-eyed at me, as if he's never seen me before.

"Cool belt," he says. "But, Granny, those glasses are rubbish!" He starts to laugh.

It's one of those days when my confidence is going to see-saw. I take another look in the interior mirror, this time with glasses. Dan's right — they are awful, with bright blue frames, a colour which doesn't suit me. Blue-tinted lenses only make matters worse. And of course, they are huge — Deirdre Barlow jobs. And even Deirdre has new modern frames now, I remind myself.

"They're only for driving," I explain to my grandson, but he's not going to change his opinion.

"They're still rubbish."

Even though I agree, I shove them on my nose and finally, we set off.

The post office is our first port of call. There's a parking space right outside — where the queue for service ends. We join it.

Inside is a small selection of greetings cards, some sweets and magazines.

Once through the door, Dan heads for the comics. I keep an eye on him while taking in the man next to me. He's rather good-looking, with a full head of hair and nice teeth. I mark him ten out of ten as he smiles at me.

He nods towards where Dan is trying to decide whether today's reading should be Bob The Builder or Ninja Turtles.

"Got your hands full there."

As a chat-up line it's not brilliant, but at least he's noticed me.

"He's at that age where he asks a million questions a day."

The stranger smiles again, no doubt thinking I'm exaggerating. I'm not, and to prove it Dan appears between us, tugging at my sweater.

"Granny, Granny."

"Granny?" When the stranger says it, there's definitely a question mark attached.

"Yes. Dan's my grandson."

The "Friend" Remembers Wartime Chanteuses & Entertainers

Dame Vera Lynn b 1917

BORN Vera Margaret Welch in East London, Dame Vera Lynn made her performance debut at seven and first sang on national radio in 1935 with the Joe Loss Orchestra.

It was while working with another bandleader, Bert Ambrose, that she met her husband, the saxophonist, Harry Lewis, who later became her manager.

Her first big hit was "The Little Boy That Santa Claus Forgot" in 1937.

Vera became known as the "Forces' Sweetheart" after "The Daily Express" ran a competition and she was voted the winner.

Her best-loved songs include "We'll Meet Again", "White Cliffs Of Dover" and "Yours". She had her own radio show during the war called "Sincerely Yours", which ran for six years. Vera also worked in Burma and North Africa entertaining the troops. At one point she was receiving over 1000 letters a week from soldiers.

Often, she used to sleep in the Criterion Theatre in the heart of Piccadilly because she had to broadcast to the overseas forces from there at two o' clock in the morning!

Her songs were real morale-boosters for "the boys", as she referred to them, fighting in far-off battlefields.

"And we're looking for a grandad," my sweet little descendant says, in all innocence. "Can you name all the Ninja Turtles?"

Panic and confusion fight in the stranger's face. An assistant magically becomes available and the failed contender in Dan's *Are You Suitable Grandad Material?* test sprints to the counter.

Dan, hands on hips, mouth set in a downward curve, slowly shakes his head. I get my post weighed, pay for the stamps and Ninja comic, and make a hasty exit.

It's because I'm aiming for such a quick get-away that I forget to put on my

Vera Lynn

She was awarded the OBE in 1969 and a DBE in 1975.

She was also presented with a Burma Star in April, 1985, to acknowledge the four-month concert she gave to soldiers there forty years previously.

A staunch supporter of charities, she is a life-long member of the WRVS and her local Women's Institute.

blue specs. We've driven halfway down the road by the time I remember and then, as we're so close to the carpark behind the market, I decide not to bother.

That's why I bump into the back of the mud-encrusted four by four ahead. There's a man sitting in the driver's seat, and I see him lurch dramatically as the front of my little car connects with the back of his.

Dan is fine.

"Oops!" is all he has to say.

The door of the car in front is thrown open, and the driver gets out. He's tall and slim. In two giant strides he's standing between the vehicles.

"Stay where you are," I tell Dan, as I tremblingly get out to face the music.

He's already shouting.

"Stupid woman!"

I teeter round to the front of my car and lose my cool. He's got a ruddy great tow-bar fitted and it's broken my number plate in two, while his oversized car is undamaged.

"What's the problem?" I ask him. "Your car's all right. I didn't see your tow-bar — that's why I bumped into you."

Dan appears at my side.

"And you didn't have your rubbish glasses on." He beams.

The four by four owner lifts an eyebrow.

"Perhaps you should wear them in future," he suggests. Then, surprisingly, he smiles. "No real harm done. It won't cost you much for a new number plate. You could try that auto-spares place on the corner of Lower Road."

21

He turns to go.

"Can you build robots?" Dan shouts at his back.

The man stops, takes a pace back and smiles falsely.

"Children should be seen, but not heard."

Dan shrugs his shoulders and slowly shakes his head.

I don't know what comes over me, but I am compelled to blow a raspberry at this miserable four-by-four-owning, child-unfriendly, definitely-not-grandad material.

Dan chuckles as he picks up my broken number plate.

"Lower Road," he reminds me.

THE auto-spares shop is easy to find. We make our way between the brightly-coloured plastic buckets filled with car shampoos, sponges, packets of spanners and all sorts of things I'll never ever want.

It's pretty dark inside. Dan lobs his half of the number plate, together with the comic he's still clutching, on to the counter.

As if he's just been catapulted through a trapdoor in the floorboards, a man pops up from the other side of the counter. His dark hair is receding at the temples. His brown eyes smile at us both.

"Oooh, Ninja Turtles," he says, picking up Dan's comic. "Leonardo's my favourite." He riffles through the pages.

"Ahem!" I try for his attention. "Could you supply me with a new number plate, please?"

"If you've got your registration document and driving licence with you?"

"No, but I can bring them in."

"Can you make robots?" Dan interrupts.

"Yes," the assistant says.

Dan smiles. Before I can stop him he's giving me the biggest red face in history.

"Do you want to be my grandad?"

The poor bloke should be as embarrassed as I am, but he's not.

"That would be up to your grandma." He laughs. His brown eyes crinkle. "But I *am* available."

"Daniel!" I only ever use my grandson's full name when he's in trouble.

"Yes?" they say in unison.

"Hey, you've got the same name as me," the other-side-of-the-counter Dan says to my Dan.

I grab my Dan's hand, ready for another quick get-away.

"You'll bring in the paperwork later?" the other Dan asks. "Please."

His smile disarms me.

"Yes," is all I can manage.

"Big Dan, Little Dan," my grandson chants as we exit.

Big Dan, Little Dan. I wonder if it's an omen? ◼

Samuel And Son

*I*T'S really quite a little place, as livery stables go,
   But Samuel Swift, proprietor, and Tom, his
bright-faced son,
Run it with such expertise that they never fail to please,
And when you need a coach and pair, they're secondary
   to none.

Tim and Toby pull the coach, old faithfuls, gentle-eyed,
Trotting up and down the road, whenever there's a call,
With Samuel perched there on his own, like a king upon
   a throne,
A driver with such dignity that he's esteemed by all.

And often, if the coach pulls up, along the village street,
Little folk will scamper through an open cottage door,
Clutching carrots crisp and sweet, for Tim and Toby's
   special treat,
With their granny close behind them, in her floral pinafore.

But today our Mr Samuel Swift works
   hard, with might and main,
For the wedding day equipage
   has to look its shining best,
So, using lots of elbow
   grease, he'll wash and
   polish and not cease
Until he's really
   satisfied — while
   young Tom does
   the rest.

With brush and curry
   comb to hand, and
   whistling like a bird,
Tom grooms old Tim and Toby —
   he will brush them till they gleam —
Knowing, when the bells ring out, the guests will cry, without
   a doubt,
"Hooray for Samuel Swift and Son — oh, what a
   splendid team!"

— *Kathleen O'Farrell*.

Isn't It Romantic?

"S O, I'll have to leave you in charge," Linda croaked over the telephone line.

"Don't worry," Emma reassured her. "I'll cope fine."

"It's just the window," Linda managed, between bouts of coughing. "I was going to do something special for Valentine's Day. But I don't think I could manage . . ."

"You stay right where you are," Emma said firmly. "I'll cope."

As she put the phone down, she couldn't help feeling mildly excited at the prospect. Of course, she was sorry for poor Linda, struck down with the 'flu. But it was a chance to do the charity shop window all on her own for Valentine's Day — now there was a challenge!

Emma didn't hesitate, and got straight to work. She looked through the stock of the charity shop to see what could be used. There were lots of artificial flowers, amongst them dark red roses. She also discovered some china — pretty and delicate china sprigged with flowers — and lots of books — romantic fiction, of course! There was even a bag full of sheet music that someone had brought in, and on leafing through it, there appeared to be a few romantic songs.

Feeling rather pleased with herself, she went into the back shop where the other volunteers were sipping coffee.

"Linda's off with 'flu," she told them.

They offered some sympathetic noises.

"So I'm going to be doing the window display for Valentine's Day," Emma went on.

"Why, that's lovely, dear," old Miss Thomas replied. Come rain or shine, she was in the shop every Monday — without fail. "We've got some really pretty dresses in — bridesmaids' dresses, I think."

She put down her cup and went to riffle through the racks.

"Yes, look!" She held up a cream chiffon dress.

"Oh, I do like that," Emma said excitedly. "It wants a hat to go with it, I think."

The volunteers started looking.

"Here, this might do." Katy held up a broad-brimmed straw hat.

"Mmm . . . we could trim it with ribbons," Emma suggested. "Red ribbons."

"Well, now I've got just the thing . . ."

Emma's window, everyone agreed, was a triumph. A mannequin wore the

24

by Anne Forsyth.

Illustration by
Adam Hook.

cream chiffon dress and the straw hat, trimmed with rose-red ribbons and flowers, and was surrounded by vases of dark red silk roses. There was an old-fashioned cake stand holding delicate china, and in front, a huge flower-print bowl filled with silk flowers. The sheet music was displayed on the music stand.

"It looks very romantic," Emma said to herself. It had been a lot of fun to do, and hopefully it would bring in the customers.

People often stopped to gaze at the window display. There was an old lady who stopped and smiled to herself, then looked into her purse.

Emma, at the till, noticed her hesitating, and opened the door.

"Can I help you?" she asked.

"It's the music." The lady was a little apologetic. "In the window. Is it for sale?"

"Everything's for sale." Emma smiled at her.

25

"'I'll Be Your Sweetheart,'" she said. "My husband used to sing that to me when we were courting."

"Oh, how romantic." Emma sighed.

"I'd like to buy it." The old lady summoned up her courage. "As a kind of memento."

"Of course." Emma climbed into the window to retrieve the music. "They're lovely words," she added, as she wrapped it carefully.

"It brings back memories," the old lady said with a smile.

"Well, that's one satisfied customer," Emma said to the rest of the volunteers.

But later on, the young couple who stopped by the window didn't look like they were going to buy a romantic souvenir. They were arguing; Emma could tell. She was glaring at him, and he scowled back at her.

Emma craned her neck so that she could see more clearly. At last the young man shrugged his shoulders and went off. Emma watched him cross the square and go into the motor spares shop immediately opposite. The girl looked as if she might be crying. Emma's heart went out to her.

Then the girl moved off in the opposite direction. They've quarrelled, Emma thought to herself. What a pity.

It had been a busy day in the shop. Lots of people had come to admire the window — and they had bought a few things, too!

LATE in the afternoon, the doorbell jangled and the young man Emma had watched earlier entered the shop.

"That bowl in the window, with the roses," he said gruffly.

"Yes?" Emma replied, looking up.

"I'll take it," he said.

"Oh, of course." Emma crawled into the window again. "She'll love it," she told the young man, wrapping the china bowl.

"Yes, well . . ." He shuffled his feet. "We had a bit of an argument . . ."

"I know," Emma said. "I saw you."

"We had some spare cash, and I wanted to go and buy a new set of spanners," he said. "We didn't have much time. She was hanging about, gazing in the window. And when I came out of the bike shop, she'd gone." He looked rather bashful.

"Well, it's a lovely present — she'll really appreciate it," Emma said firmly.

The last customer that afternoon was a thin, rather gawky schoolgirl.

"That dress . . ." she said abruptly.

"Yes, dear?" Old Miss Thomas was behind the counter. "The cream one with lace?"

"What size?" The girl didn't seem to have heard of the word "please".

"A twelve, I think." Miss Thomas peered into the window.

"I'll get it," Emma put in quickly. "Would you like to try it on?"

The girl nodded.

Again, her back aching, Emma crawled into the window.

"The fitting room's through the back . . ."

It was astonishing how different the girl looked in the dress. In jeans and a black sweater she had seemed plain, her dark hair hanging lank over her collar.

Now she stood up straight and revolved slowly in front of the mirror. Suddenly she smiled.

"Oh, it's awfully pretty," she said. "I'll take it!"

"For a special occasion?" Emma asked casually as she wrapped the dress.

"I saved my Christmas money," the girl replied. "It's for the school dance."

"Well, you're going to look lovely," Emma assured her.

The girl turned at the door.

"Thank you," she said. "Thank you very much."

"Fancy that!" Emma said to Miss Thomas and Katy. "We've done really well with that window."

It had been quite a long day, though, and soon she was feeling rather tired.

"You go," she told the other volunteers. "You've been marvellous. And I hope Linda will be back in a day or two." She smiled to herself. "I'll tidy up and lock up."

When they had gone, she looked at the window; she'd need to re-do it tomorrow. It had been a successful day, but how tired she was — and her back ached with all that crawling around.

Bother Valentine's Day, she thought crossly. It was just another bonanza for the shops. Bother hearts and flowers. Bother red roses. Bother romance. Oh, well. It was all over for another year. She just had time to catch the bus home.

Emma put on her jacket and thick woollen scarf, and glanced in the mirror. I'm just a tired, middle-aged woman, she thought, long past romance.

Just then, the doorbell jangled.

"I'm sorry — we're closed," she said, without looking up.

"Hello, Emma."

"Oh, Mike!" Emma stared at her husband. "What are you doing here? Is there something wrong?"

"Calm down. There's nothing wrong," he reassured her.

"You just caught me," she said reproachfully. "I was going for the bus."

"No need to," he said. "I've brought the car. Can't have you going on the bus — not on a cold winter's evening like this. Come on, let's get off home. The kids have laid the table for you. Not without a bit of an argument, I may say," he added with a grin. "They've tidied up, too. Surprise, surprise! And we'll pick up the fish and chips on the way back."

"Fish and chips — just what I feel like." Emma smiled. "But what's all this in aid of?" she asked, puzzled.

"It's Valentine's Day!" Mike replied with a grin.

"Well, now, so it is," Emma said thoughtfully, as she locked the door behind her. ■

C OME on, puss, there's a good boy," I whisper encouragingly across the garden.

It's late at night, cold, dark and damp. The rain has stopped, but the drips from the trees are finding their way inside my collar. A car door slams. Why can't people do that quietly? They'll frighten him.

Several weeks ago, a ginger cat started appearing in the back garden. Painfully thin, eyes almost stuck together, and his ears a mess, he was a pitiful sight.

I bought some cat food, spooned it into an old bowl and left it in the garden, close to the conifer tree where I'd seen him lying. Standing at my kitchen window, I watched until he dragged himself weakly across the lawn to the food.

Animal Magic

Illustration by Vedel-Roberty.

by June Killham.

28

Liz, in the flat below mine, named him Bert, and we've managed to feed him regularly. He's wary of humans, only venturing into the open when he's sure nobody's there.

The trouble is that Liz has now moved out. A new tenant is due to arrive any day and I don't know if she — or he, or they — will tolerate our Bert. So I decided to buy an old cat travelling basket from the charity shop, leave it in the garden near a large bush, and put his food close by.

Each night I've placed the bowl nearer and nearer to the basket; now it's just inside. And I'm kneeling behind the bush, waiting for Bert to be enticed into my trap. He's underneath a shrub at the opposite end of the garden and I've been here, lurking with intent, for almost an hour. I'm getting cramp.

Stretching my limbs slowly and quietly, I flex my neck, turn my head from side to side — and then stifle the scream which rises in my throat.

Close behind me stand a pair of large masculine shoes. They don't move. My eyes travel up a pair of blue jeans and a black sweatshirt, to a stern face.

"Good evening." I gulp softly, not wanting to alarm Bert.

"Is it?"

"A bit damp, actually."

"Now we've dispensed with the meteorological formalities, may I enquire what you are doing?" he asks icily.

Relieved that he doesn't sound like a homicidal maniac — though thankfully I've no experience of what a homicidal maniac is supposed to sound like — I relax slightly.

"Well, I don't know you." I smile. "Perhaps I ought to ask what you're doing."

"I shall be moving into the ground floor flat of this house tomorrow, and I have shared use of the garden with the tenant in the upstairs flat," he informs me curtly. My heart sinks.

"That's me. I live upstairs."

"Do you?" He walks away.

I glance at the bush opposite. There's no sign of a cat.

*　　*　　*　　*

A few minutes after arriving home from work the following evening, I'm in the garden again. First impressions can be completely wrong. I must have looked highly suspicious last night, and the poor man was probably stressed out with the hassle of moving. But, in case my new neighbour doesn't overflow with kindness and compassion where stray cats are concerned, I urgently need to deal with Bert.

I put some smelly, tempting sardines in the basket. If he didn't eat anything yesterday, perhaps today he'll be hungry enough to risk putting his nose inside.

I take up position behind the bush and, half an hour later, my patience is rewarded. Belly low on the floor, Bert makes his way cautiously and slowly over to the basket. He steps inside and starts to eat the sardines.

Stealthily I creep forward, push the door shut and fasten the strap.

Realising he's captive terrifies him. He twists round and round, frantically hurling himself from side to side in the basket. Alarmed he's going to hurt himself, I rush indoors, and up to my flat.

I put the basket on the lounge floor, undo the strap, and step back. A ginger cannonball hurtles out of the basket and rushes round the room. My standard lamp falls over with a loud crash, books fly off shelves, and a small coffee table topples over. Howling and wailing, Bert dashes into the kitchen.

The doorbell rings. Oh, no.

Unless it's an emergency, there's no way that door's being opened. I can't risk Bert making a bid for freedom.

"Yes?" I bellow through the letter-box. "How can I help you?"

"We met yesterday in the garden," a terse voice informs me. "My name is Phillip Shelbourn. I was hoping for a quiet, relaxing evening."

"Oh. Hello." Totally flustered, I'm not sure why he's bothered to come upstairs and tell me his plans for the remainder of the day.

"Is the dreadful noise you're making a regular occurrence, or merely a Friday evening ritual?" he asks.

There's another loud crash from the kitchen. What is Bert doing? He could hurt himself. And he must be terrified. I just don't have time to explain the noise to Mr Shelbourn.

"I'm sorry, but I'm ever so busy," I yell. "Was there anything else?"

Angry muttering is followed by a curt reply.

"Nothing whatsoever."

I run back to the kitchen. Bert is hiding behind the washing machine. Clearly he feels safer in the dark, where he can't see any frightening new things. I chew my bottom lip, wondering what to do next.

Sitting on the floor beside the washing machine, I talk to him gently. But no amount of coaxing is going to persuade him to come out. I don't know how long we stay there, but the room grows dark. I don't stir to switch on the light. My eyelids droop.

"I'll have to go to bed, Bert." I yawn. "Don't worry. Nobody can hurt you here, I promise."

Reaching slowly behind the machine, I come into contact with his chin. I stroke it gently. He responds by pushing against my hand.

Blinking back an emotional tear, I put a bowl of food on the floor along with a saucer of milk, and another of water. I find a cardboard box, stuff an old jumper into it, and place it beside the saucers. Then I make a milky drink and take myself off to bed, silently closing the kitchen door behind me. I'm cleaning my teeth when a thought hits me.

What if he needs to go to the toilet during the night?

Rummaging round for another cardboard box, I line it with a black bin liner. Hastily pulling an old anorak over my nightie, I shove my feet into a pair of sturdy walking boots.

Clutching a torch and a trowel and feeling ridiculous, I trudge down to the garden. As I dig up earth to fill the cardboard box, I have a notion I'm being watched.

Realising how vulnerable I am, I glance anxiously over my shoulder, but no-one is there. I step on to the footpath and I walk back round towards the front door.

Phillip Shelbourn is staring out of his lounge window, shaking his head.

I chuckle to myself. The poor man probably has huge misgivings about having chosen to live in the flat beneath me. I'll knock on his door tomorrow, introduce myself properly, and tell him what I've been doing.

ARLY next morning I tiptoe into the kitchen. The food bowl and the saucer are empty, and Bert is lying in the makeshift bed. Tentatively I stroke his head. The soft purr is music to my ears.

I pay a speedy visit to the local petshop, staggering back with a cat bed, cat food, cat litter and litter tray, two ping-pong balls and a catnip mouse.

Putting down more milk and food, I step back to give Bert space. He limps painfully over to the bowl, and I gasp at the large gaping wound on his leg.

Donning a pair of thick gloves, and taking a deep breath, I pounce from behind and shove him unceremoniously into the cat basket. Hissing and spitting, Bert lashes out as I fasten the strap.

I pick up the basket in one hand and my purse and keys in the other and hurry down the stairs.

The door of the downstairs flat opens. I groan to myself. Now is not a good time for those explanations.

My new neighbour glowers.

"What are you doing to that unfortunate animal?" he demands.

Bert is yowling like a banshee, and looking at me with loathing.

"Nothing dreadful, don't worry. He just hates being in the basket."

I rush out of the entrance hall.

As I walk the couple of streets to the veterinary surgery, I begin to wonder if I'm destined unwittingly to annoy my new neighbour every time I see him. However, I'm glad he was concerned by Bert's cries. There are some unbelievably cruel people around and, for all Mr Shelbourn knows, I could be one of them.

When it's our turn to see the vet, the first thing I learn is that Bert needs to be renamed Bertha.

The newly christened cat is given a thorough examination. Then she's vaccinated, and the wound on her back leg cleaned and treated.

"She's obviously been living rough for a while," the vet observes, "but her overall health isn't that bad. There are no problems we can't cope with."

Bertha seems far less distressed. The fear and bewilderment haven't left her eyes, but she's probably feeling more comfortable. Halfway home, laden down with drops for her ears, cream for her eyes, worm pills and antibiotics for the leg wound, I notice the strap fastening on the basket is working loose. I put my arms round the basket, clutching it closely to me.

"Please don't try and escape," I plead with her.

When I reach the main front door I can't risk putting my precious cargo down. But my keys are deep in the back pocket of my trousers. Reluctantly, I press my elbow against the downstairs flat's doorbell.

Dripping water, wearing a towelling dressing-gown and a scowl, Phillip Shelbourn answers the door.

"Thanks ever so much."

I brush hurriedly past him, into the safety of the hall.

"The fact that you don't have a key to the main front door is somewhat inconvenient for the other tenant, isn't it?" Mr Shelbourn's voice is tinged with more than a little sarcasm.

I decide to give him the full unabridged story of Bert and Bertha. Shivering, and occasionally nodding, he listens attentively.

"Of course, you could have put the basket down, with the strap firmly against the wall, and then retrieved your keys," he points out.

Why didn't I think of that? A blush creeps up my face and I climb the stairs, apologising, and mumbling something over my shoulder about not normally being so stupid.

BERTHA and I rapidly become friends. She's a character, and I can't imagine life without her — although there are certain aspects of cat ownership I'd been blissfully unaware of.

She jumps on the table and almost lands in my meal when I'm eating. She chases flies on the windows, which means the net curtains are in shreds, the window-sills are empty and my dustbin is full of broken ornaments.

I wake up with a heavy weight squashing my chest, and a rough wet tongue lavishing watery affection on the end of my nose.

I don't grow as close to my new neighbour as I do to my cat, but there are no further misunderstandings between us. When we meet, we always talk.

Phillip's a serious man, intelligent, and well-read. He does sometimes come across as a bit off-hand, even rude, but that seems to be his way of hiding the

Ballycastle, Co. Antrim

PLACED on the most north-easterly tip of County Antrim, Northern Ireland, Ballycastle is surrounded with breathtaking beauty and steeped in cultural history. This small rural seaside town is best known for the "Ould Lammas Fair", probably the largest of its kind in Ireland with its "dulse" and "yellowman". Nearby is one of the world's great natural wonders, the famous Giant's Causeway.

J. CAMPBELL KERR.

fact he's basically a shy, insecure person. He's thoughtful, though, and never forgets to ask after Bertha.

"I think she's well enough to start going out," I tell him one morning. "But with me being upstairs, I won't know when she wants to come back in."

"I'll let her in the main door, whenever I see her."

"That's kind. Thank you." I'm grateful.

The next evening, Bertha's on my lap, purring like a smooth-running engine, when we're disturbed by hammering from downstairs, followed by the sound of sawing, and loud drilling.

Bertha stops purring, and her tail swishes from side to side. She's still nervous and timid. Unusual noises startle her. It's my turn to complain.

Going downstairs, I find Phillip on his knees and a square hole in the bottom panel of the main door.

"I contacted the landlord," he says. "I told him about Bertha and he said it was all right to put in a cat-flap, so long as I restored the door to its original state before moving out."

I'm speechless.

"I love cats." His face creases slightly into a bashful smile, which makes him look completely different.

PHILLIP finishes installing the cat-flap. Bertha doesn't appear to have encountered one before, and investigates it with a feline frown. We try to show her how it works. It's not long before we're both giggling childishly. It's difficult not to when your head's poking through a cat-flap.

Despite all our efforts, Bertha remains puzzled.

"Didn't Christopher Robin say that Pooh was a bear of very little brain? I think I've got a cat of very little brain." I chuckle.

Bertha stalks away, glancing reproachfully over her shoulder. She sits down, sticks one of her hind legs up in the air and proceeds to wash it.

Laughing, Phillip and I turn to each other. Our eyes hold, my heartbeat increases rapidly, and my stomach starts doing peculiar things. Lowering my gaze, I try to convince myself I must have picked up a virus.

Spring slips into glorious summer. Bertha doesn't master the intricacies of the cat-flap, but uses it as a knocking device instead. Phillip hears it, lets her in, and then carries her upstairs to my door, where we become accustomed to having a long chat. Bertha usually weaves in out and out of our legs, and rubs up against us.

I start inviting Phillip in for coffee. Some evenings we cook for each other.

Now it's winter. Bitter winds are blowing across the garden, rain hurls against the windows. Bertha prefers to stay indoors, and she won't be happy tomorrow when we take her to the cattery.

But Phillip and I know she'll be purring with delight when we come back from honeymoon, and the three of us move into our own house. ■

Just The Ticket!

Illustration by Sally Rowe.

by Lisa
Main.

GRAN,
do you have
anything for our
raffle?" Simon
asked between mouthfuls of
freshly-baked gingerbread.

"What raffle would that be,
then?" Isabel gave him a
knowing smile. Simon had
talked about almost
nothing but

Boys' Brigade since he'd joined a few weeks earlier, and she knew they had a coffee morning coming up in a couple of weeks' time.

"At Brigade," he said, confirming her suspicions. "Mr Moore says we'll make lots of money if we have some nice prizes on the table."

"I'm sure I can find something . . ." Isabel remembered Walter Moore. He'd been very kind when Ron had died some years earlier, and he was popular with all the boys in his company. "I'll make some gingerbread for the teas as well," she added.

"Wicked!"

Isabel recalled that this was a compliment in the eyes of today's youth.

"You make great gingerbread, Gran! Everyone will want to buy it."

That evening, Isabel started to look for a suitable raffle prize. There was the box of bath salts she'd received last Christmas from a friend who didn't know that she preferred taking showers. The Brigade was welcome to those, but they were hardly the exciting kind of prize to boost ticket sales!

Then she remembered the vase Ron had inherited from an uncle not long after they married. Ron told her he'd always admired it as a boy and had given it pride of place in the tiny lounge of their first flat. Isabel had never been able to find the heart to tell Ron she thought it was the ugliest thing she'd ever seen.

However, over the years and with each house move, she'd managed to find it a slightly less prominent home; first in the dining-room, then the spare room. It rested now in the hall cupboard in a box she hadn't unpacked since moving into her new flat.

After a few minutes rummaging about in the box, Isabel found a shape that resembled the vase and began to unwrap the layers of paper around it. There it was in all its garish glory. Isabel wrinkled her nose as she wiped away a fine layer of dust and looked at the blaze of enamelled colours that merged and blended over the surface of the vase.

The years hadn't tempered her dislike of it, but it was in excellent condition and on the TV programme she watched about antiques, they'd said that ornaments of this kind were becoming popular again.

Perhaps someone would like it. There was no doubt that it would be a striking addition to the raffle prize table.

"You should be in a home where you're loved," she told the vase as she carefully wrapped it up again. "Everything deserves that much."

THE church hall was already busy when Isabel arrived at the coffee morning. She visited the craft stall and waved to her daughter-in-law, who'd been roped in to help serve the teas and looked rushed off her feet.

"Gran, come and buy some tickets." She heard her grandson's voice and turned round to see that he was helping with the raffle.

The table was laden with prizes and there in the middle of them all and sitting on top of a small plinth, was the vase. The sun was shining in through the window and reflecting off the surface.

"I'll take two strips," she told Simon, "just as long as I don't win that vase back again."

"I really can't understand why you wouldn't want to." Walter Moore had come to stand beside her. "It's a real work of art. Ticket sales are double what they usually are because so many people like it. I wanted to thank you personally for being generous enough to donate it to us."

"It really was nothing," Isabel assured him, and he laughed.

"Well, there's no accounting for taste. Speaking of which, Simon tells me that you've made the 'best gingerbread in the universe' for our tea stall. Will you join me for a cup of coffee while I sample it?"

"I'm afraid that Simon might have exaggerated a little bit," she said with a smile. "I hope you won't be disappointed."

"I'm sure I won't be."

Walter took her arm and guided her to an empty table.

"How are you?" he asked when they were waiting for their refreshments to arrive.

"I'm very well, thank you."

"Simon tells me you've moved house recently."

"Yes." Isabel found herself wondering just how much Simon had told Walter about her. "I found that the house was far too big and I couldn't really cope with the garden after I lost Ron."

"I know exactly what you mean. I haven't felt the same in my place since Maria died, but unlike you I haven't found the courage to move away. Of course I have my hobbies and the Brigade keeps me busy, but some nights when I go home to an empty house I feel so lonely, even now."

"That's only natural."

He'd sounded so desolate that Isabel reached out to lay her hand over his in a gesture of comfort.

"I feel the same way, too."

For a few seconds they were both silent and neither made any attempt to move their hand, but then the drinks arrived and the air of empathy between them was broken.

"Let me assure you Simon didn't exaggerate," Walter said a little later. "This really is the best gingerbread in the universe!"

"Oh, you're just flattering me," Isabel protested, but she really didn't mind.

"Isabel." Walter suddenly looked awkward. "I don't suppose you'd like to go out for tea with me one Sunday afternoon? We could have a walk first if you'd like."

"I think I'd like that very much."

"So would I."

Walter looked as if he was about to say more, but at that moment the loudspeaker crackled into life.

"Ladies and gentlemen, please get out your raffle tickets. It's time for the grand draw!"

ARTHUR MALONE was about to get off the bus when a lady called him back.

"You've left your parcel."

"Oh, thank you."

He picked the package up and tried to look more grateful than he really felt. He would have been quite happy to leave the thing there for someone else. There had been a useful-looking fishing reel among the prizes on the raffle table and he'd bought extra tickets in the hope of winning it.

Instead, he'd ended up with this vase. He supposed it was nice enough as far as vases went, but it wasn't a thing he had any use for.

"First prize," the Boys' Brigade Captain had said as he'd handed it to him. "How lucky you are."

Arthur didn't feel very lucky. In the past few months life had been full of disappointments and winning this vase instead of the fishing reel was just another one to add to the list.

When he reached his house he let himself in and checked the doormat for letters. There were none, nor were there any messages on his answering machine. Of course, it was unlikely that there would have been a message.

Most of the companies he'd applied to didn't work on Saturdays, but he'd hoped that one of them might have put a letter in the post the day before. If he was going to get an interview with any of them, he should have heard by now.

"But you're not going to hear," he said aloud to himself. "They think you're past it. You're on the scrapheap, Arthur, old boy, and you might as well get used to it."

The trouble was that he didn't want to get used to it. He didn't feel any older than he had when he'd started working for Halliday & Sons as a junior book-keeper all those years ago. Besides, if sixty was the new forty, as everyone kept telling him, then at fifty-nine he should still be seen as in his prime!

Of course he hadn't been. When Hallidays had been forced to make cutbacks five months earlier, he'd been among the first to receive redundancy. Not that they'd called it that.

"Early retirement," Michael Halliday had said with a smile that Arthur had seen as dismissive. "You deserve it after all these years of loyal service. Think of all the time you'll have to go fishing."

38

Gentle Beauty

THEY'VE come here from
  her shop on Market
Square,
Miss Melrose, with her
  helper, Albert
  Brown,
To make this little
  church look twice as
  fair,
And Albert, as he sets
  the basket down,
Knows he'll enjoy
  the task, though
  it takes hours,
For he has such
  affinity with
  flowers.

Nothing
  disturbs
  them in the
  friendly
  gloom
Of this quiet
  place, where peace hangs on the air,
The flowers spill out in splendour, their perfume
Seems like a blessing, or a silent prayer.
Only the snip, snip, snip of scissors, or a word
Of praise, from Margaret Melrose, can be heard.

For Albert, knowing she relies on him,
Finds nothing too much trouble. Tirelessly,
He answers to her needs, her every whim,
For this, for that, fern, flowers or greenery,
Knowing the end result, a work of art,
Will bring great satisfaction to his heart.

For Albert, in his work, will always find
A gentle beauty, of the lasting kind.

— *Kathleen O'Farrell.*

No-one had bothered to ask Arthur if he'd wanted to retire, he thought morosely as he went to put the kettle on. That had been a nice piece of gingerbread he'd had at the Brigade coffee morning. He wished he'd thought to buy some more for tea-time.

While the kettle was boiling, he went out to the greenhouse and checked his tomatoes. There was going to be a good crop this year. Next time he was in the library he would look for a book with a recipe for chutney in it. The Angling Club could sell it at their Christmas Fayre.

There were no flowers in the tiny back garden. Arthur had never been one for fripperies like that. He was a practical man. Organisation and method meant everything to him — or at least they had when he'd been working. He sighed and went back into the house just as the kettle started to whistle.

Things could have been worse, he mused, as he spooned tea into the pot. His settlement from Hallidays had been generous. Along with his savings, that meant he didn't have to worry about money, and at least he had his hobbies. But that was all they were — just filling in time . . .

When he was younger, his brother had joked that Arthur would never marry because he was already wedded to his work. That had proved to be true, and now that he had lost his job he was bereft. Without a reason to get up and go out in the morning his days had lost their sense of purpose.

He was doing his best to keep busy. That was why he'd gone to the coffee morning after doing his shopping. It had helped to pass another hour.

"And I won a vase." He wondered if he should be worried about his new habit of talking to himself since he'd lost his job. "Well, it can go to the charity shop on Monday morning. Someone who wants it might as well have the chance of owning it."

*   *   *   *

The lady in the charity shop looked harassed when Arthur joined the queue at her counter, and she sighed when he held up the bag containing the vase and some books he'd read.

"Oh, dear, more donations." She flushed and quickly corrected herself. "Sorry. I didn't mean it to sound like that. It's just that we're very short staffed at the moment. Do you think you could pop them through in the back shop for me? I'd be ever so grateful."

"Don't you want to log them in or something so you know what you've got?" Arthur asked.

The assistant gave another sigh.

"We rarely know what we've got. To be honest, it takes all our time just to keep the customers served and the shelves stocked."

Arthur thought this sounded like a very poor arrangement, and when he opened the door of the back shop and saw the chaos of plastic bags and bulging bin liners piled up against the wall, he was shocked.

"You need a system," he told the assistant when he went back to the counter. "All that stuff out there wants sorting, grading and listing. Then when you do a stock-take you'll know exactly what's been sold and be able to tally it with your takings."

"I'm afraid we also need the time to do something like that and we simply don't have it," the woman replied wearily. "What you're talking about sounds like a full-time job and no-one's going to do that as a volunteer, are they?"

"I would." The words came out of Arthur's mouth before he realised it himself. "I'd be no good at selling but I could come in and do the books and things for you. I'm very good at book-keeping and I'm still in my prime, you know."

Arthur soon found out he'd been wrong about his lack of skill as a salesman. When he wasn't in the back keeping his immaculate stock-room up to date, he came to enjoy working in the shop. He even helped the young lad who came in looking for a present for his girlfriend.

"What about this vase then?" Arthur asked. "So happens I handed it in myself. I bet it'd look right pretty on her window-sill with some flowers in it."

I HATE Roddy Clarke and I never want to see him again."

Katie Lassiter slammed the front door of her house and pounded up the stairs to her bedroom, where she threw herself down on the bed and started to cry. How could Roddy humiliate her like that? She'd thought he really *cared*. After all, they'd been going out together for almost two months and he'd given her that beautiful vase for her birthday only two weeks earlier.

How could he have kissed Jade behind the science block? Jade was always after other girls' boyfriends, but Katie had truly believed that Roddy would be true to her.

"Katie?" Her mother's voice was followed by a tentative tap on the bedroom door. "I've brought you a snack. Can I come in?"

"I s'pose so."

Katie sat up as Sally Lassiter entered the room with a tray.

"Hot chocolate and biscuits, just the thing for a broken heart."

"That's not funny." Katie sniffed.

"I wasn't trying to be." Sally put down the tray and went to sit at her daughter's side. "I know it feels dreadful right now, but believe me, it really isn't as bad as you think. You're still so very young."

"I'm sixteen," Katie protested.

"Exactly." Sally smiled tenderly at her. "It's much too early to be pining over one boy."

Katie grimaced. Any minute now Mum would trot out that old "plenty of fish in the sea" cliché and she didn't think she could bear that. Why didn't anyone understand that she was in love with Roddy and that there could never be anyone else like him?

"You don't know how it feels," she muttered, and to her annoyance, Sally laughed.

"Oh, Katie, you silly, darling girl, of course I do." Sally's eyes grew distant. "Kevin Turley, captain of the sixth form football team. I was utterly devoted to him. I never missed a match and spent the entire time cheering him on. I kept every report from the school magazine that mentioned him and I slept with the team photo under my pillow every night for a year."

"Did he two-time you as well?"

Katie was fascinated by

The "Friend" Remembers Wartime Chanteuses & Entertainers

Petula Clark CBE b 1932

PETULA CLARK has had an amazing career as a singer and entertainer over the years.

"Our Pet" was born in Epsom, Surrey, and began her career as a child singer, entertaining the troops during World War II. She even had her own radio series, "Pet's Parlour", in 1943.

Encouraged by her parents, Petula found radio stardom on shows like "Variety Band Box" and participated in hundreds of performances for the Allied troops, earning her the nickname "The Forces' Girl".

She made her film debut in "Medal For The General" in 1944 and appeared in many more subsequently. In 1968 she starred alongside Fred Astaire in the musical "Finian's Rainbow" and recorded the classic song, "Look To The Rain".

Sustaining a career as an adult, she became one of Britain's most successful pop singers, earning ten gold discs, two Grammy awards and a string of international hits including "Downtown" in 1964 and "My Love" in 1966.

She had an international Number One in 1967 with "This Is My Song", written by Charlie Chaplin.

this hitherto unknown aspect of her mother's past.

"Oh, no." Sally shook her head. "We never dated. I don't think he even knew I existed, but that didn't mean that the feelings I had for him weren't real and painful. I spent the entire summer term hoping he'd ask me to the Leavers' Ball, but he didn't. He asked one of my friends instead and I thought I could never be happy again. I couldn't bear to see him with my friend so I didn't go to the Ball."

She smiled ruefully.

"I wish I had, now. I missed one of the best nights of the year! Then I went to university, met a lot of new friends, including your dad, and realised that Kevin hadn't been that great, after all. I know it's hard to believe now, but one day you'll feel the same way about Roddy."

Petula Clark

Later in her career, she appeared in "Blood Brothers" on Broadway and "Sunset Boulevard", which opened in London in 1995, then went on to tour the USA.

Petula was awarded the CBE in 1998.

She is still one of Britain's all time biggest-selling female recording artists with over 70 million sales.

"But I love him," Katie wailed.

"And he'll probably always have a special place in your heart. First love always does. But the hurt will go away, I promise you."

Sally bent forward to kiss her daughter's forehead.

"I wish I could make it better for you now, but I'm afraid only time can do that. Time — and hot chocolate."

She stood up.

"Have you got any homework?"

"Yes. I've got to write a story for that stupid inter-school writing competition."

"Why don't you make a start then? It'll help to keep your mind off things."

When her mother had gone, Katie took her English jotter, slumped at her desk and bit miserably into a biscuit.

How was she supposed to write anything when she was suffering so much? The vase Roddy had given her was sitting on the desk with her pens in it. He'd written *love from Roddy* on the card that came with it.

Had he already been stealing away for kisses from Jade when he wrote it? Katie suddenly felt very angry. She'd been betrayed and she wanted revenge. She would write a story all right. It would be a murder mystery and the victim, who would just happened to be a two-timing cheat, would meet his demise when some unknown hand dropped a vase on his head!

✳   ✳   ✳   ✳

"I hope you all enjoyed hearing the winning story. Now I would like to invite the author, Miss Katie Lassiter, to come up and collect her prize."

43

Katie thought she could hear her parents' cheers above all the others as the mayor shook her hand and gave her a book token.

"An excellent piece of fiction, my dear. Perhaps you'll be the next Agatha Christie."

The town hall had laid on a buffet for the prize-winners and their families after the awards ceremony. Katie's parents met someone they knew, and while they were caught up in what seemed like a boring conversation about holidays she decided to go and get herself a glass of lemonade.

"Great story," the boy standing behind her in the queue said. "I never would have guessed that the cat did it by accident."

"Thank you." Katie turned and recognised another of the prize-winners, a tall boy of roughly her own age, who was dressed completely in black and had his hair dyed to match. "I liked your poem, too. It was really unusual compared to all the others."

"Yeah, well, I don't do nature and stuff. I want to write about real life as it is." He ran a hand through his floppy dark fringe and Katie thought he looked just like Heathcliff in "Wuthering Heights".

"You don't go to my school, do you?" she asked.

"No, I'm at Hartfield Academy across the town. I'm Tom." He gave a shy grin. "Maybe we could meet up in town next Saturday? There's a poetry exhibition on at the library."

Katie grinned back.

"OK, and will you bring some more of yours? I'd love to read them."

O H, Katie, this is so pretty. Are you sure you want to hand it in?" Louise Wilkes looked at the vase her pupil had handed in for the school tombola.

"Yeah. It doesn't suit my room any more. I'm painting it black and having silver accessories."

"A change of image, then?"

The room wasn't the only thing to have undergone a change since the night of the awards ceremony, Louise thought. Katie herself was looking very different these days.

"Please make sure you remove the black lipstick and eyeliner before assembly," she said firmly as she added the vase to the collection of prizes behind her desk.

On the day of the school fête, Louise went to the tombola as soon as she was able to take a short break from the bric-à-brac stall. To her delight the vase was still there with number 205 stuck to the front of it.

"I'll take ten tickets, please."

"Ten?" An arm went round her shoulders. "That's a bit extreme, isn't it? I thought we were saving up to get married."

"Hello, Shaun." Louise turned to kiss her fiancé, much to the amusement of a group of first years who were standing nearby. "I know we're not supposed to be spending too much money, but I really like that vase. One of my tutor group handed it in. I was tempted then to make a donation and keep it, but I thought that wouldn't be fair so now I'm trying to win it."

Louise started opening her tickets and was disappointed when number 205 wasn't among them.

"I'd better get back to my stall. Come round tonight. I'll make a curry and you can help me drink this."

She held up the bottle of wine that one of her tickets had won and Shaun laughed.

"We'd better enjoy it then, because after all the money you've spent on those tickets it's probably the most expensive bottle of wine I'll ever have drunk."

That evening when Shaun arrived at Louise's flat he put a carrier bag into her hands.

"For you."

"And you tell me not to spend money!" Louise tried to sound disapproving but she was secretly happy to get a present, and when she saw what was in the bag her smile deepened.

"It's the vase. Shaun, darling, thank you! But how did you get it?"

"By investing in another twenty tickets." Shaun took her in his arms. "But if I'd had to I'd have bought them all to make you happy."

"I do love you, Shaun Bell." Louise kissed him. "Now come through to the kitchen and I'll put the rice on."

Later that evening, as they both curled up on the sofa watching the TV and sipping coffee, Louise sighed.

"What's wrong?" Shaun asked.

"Nothing, really. I was just thinking. I wish we could get married sooner."

"I know, so do I." Now Shaun sighed. "But it's going to take us at least another year to save up to buy a house, and there's all the other expense. There's no point rushing into it and then being miserable because we're completely broke, is there?"

"I suppose not."

Louise didn't think she could ever be miserable as long as she was with Shaun but she supposed he was right. It was just that they'd already been engaged for a year and another twelve months more seemed like such a long time. She suppressed another sigh and picked up the TV guide.

"That antiques show is coming on. Shall we watch it?"

A few minutes later they were both laughing at the estimate given to a dismal-looking painting of a jug with a broken handle.

"They're kidding," Shaun said. "I wouldn't have given a quid for it myself."

"That's because you have no taste," Louise retorted.

Shaun snatched up a cushion and she thought he was going to throw it at her, but his arm suddenly froze and he began to stare at the screen.

"Louise, look at that vase. It's just like yours. Turn the sound up, quick."

"At a conservative estimate you should insure this item for at least fifty thousand pounds."

The reaction of the crowd on the television show was drowned out by Louise's gasp and Shaun's sharp intake of breath.

"Fifty thousand," he repeated slowly. "Think what we could do with fifty thousand pounds!"

"We could get married right away."

"In the Caribbean if we wanted."

Shaun leapt to his feet.

"Let's have another look at that vase.'

The next day Shaun borrowed his brother's car and he and Louise drove to the next town with the vase.

"The antiques shop here is one of the best," Shaun said as they walked along the High Street. "Just think, in a few minutes all our problems could be over."

"I know." Louise was as excited as he sounded. At last her dreams of marrying Shaun would come true. Why, then, was she aware of a tiny twinge of sadness as they handed the vase over to the antiques dealer for his inspection?

The man's eyes lit up as he took the vase into his steady grasp.

"This is a very exciting find. How did you come by it?"

"We won it at a school fête. Then last night we saw the one just like it on the TV." Shaun was watching the man's every movement intently.

The dealer continued to examine the vase for several more agonising minutes, then slowly shook his head and gave it back to Shaun.

"I'm afraid this is a copy. A very good copy, but not the genuine article. At auction it would raise less than twenty pounds."

✳   ✳   ✳   ✳

"I can't believe it," Shaun muttered for at least the fourth time later that afternoon as they sat in the park.

"Never mind." Louise held out the plastic container she'd brought with her. "I made your favourite egg sandwiches for you."

She was trying to sound more cheerful than she felt. For a few wonderful hours she'd thought that she and Shaun would finally be able to get married, and now the dream had been snatched away again.

"I was planning to take you out for a slap-up meal tonight, not eat egg sandwiches."

Shaun took one anyway.

"Well, look on the bright side." Louise was determined to find something to be happy about. "I've still got my vase."

"Your worthless vase," Shaun pointed out.

"It's not worthless." Louise felt a sudden surge of emotion rush through her. "At least, it's not worthless to me. You tried so hard to win it because you knew I liked it, and that makes it priceless as far as I'm concerned."

She leapt to her feet as the words poured out of her.

"And I'll tell you something else. I don't care about living in a big new house or having all the latest gadgets in the kitchen. It's *you* I want, not a lifestyle! I'd much rather get married tomorrow and live in my little rented flat together than have to wait any longer. I love you and all I want is to be your wife."

A duck quacked loudly when she'd finished speaking but Shaun was silent for several seconds.

"I wanted everything to be perfect for you," he said eventually. "You deserve the best."

"I've already got that." Louise sat down again. "I've got you. That's all I need."

"I see." Shaun seemed to be deep in thought for a minute and Louise couldn't read his expression.

She wondered if she'd hurt his feelings with her outburst.

"Well." When he finally spoke he looked no less serious. "I think we'd better go and have a word with Reverend Jones tomorrow and see how soon he can fit us in for a wedding then, don't you?"

The wedding was a simple affair but Louise knew she would always remember it as one of the happiest days of her life. The tiny reception was held in their flat and, although it was a bit of a squeeze, their friends and family didn't seem to mind. Everyone contributed a dish to the buffet and Shaun's mum had made them a beautifully-iced cake.

It sat in the centre of the table next to where the bride's posy of pink roses had been carefully arranged in a bright, multi-coloured and much-loved vase. ■

Plain Sailing!

CHARLIE hadn't thought things could get much worse. What was supposed to be a romantic summer picnic on the boating lake had turned into a nightmare. Gemma had let him down at the last minute — nothing unusual there — but he'd been perversely determined to come anyway.

Unfortunately he'd already grounded the rowing boat twice, once by the bank and once some rocks in the centre of the lake. The second time, in the process of freeing it, he'd sprained his ankle and it was swelling rapidly.

Worst of all, the boat, which had been taking on water for a while, appeared to be sinking.

He looked at the bank and wondered how near he could get before he sank completely. Not quite near enough, he suspected.

Still, he was going to have to try. The lake wasn't deep. He could get out and wade the last bit. That's if you could wade on one foot! His ankle hurt like mad. He doubted he could put any weight on it.

Rowing was much more difficult than it looked on TV. Every muscle ached and his progress wasn't helped by the rapidly rising water level in the boat. He was puffing so much that at first he didn't hear the voice behind him.

"I said, excuse me, but do you need some help?"

He didn't dare stop rowing, but he glanced round and found himself looking into amused grey eyes in a face he'd have found attractive under normal circumstances.

"No. I'm fine."

"You don't look fine. Your boat's sinking."

"Is it really? Well, thank you very much for pointing that out. I did wonder why my jeans were a wee bit damp."

He expected that to be the end of it. No woman was going to hang around after such an unchivalrous rejection, but he was too cross and humiliated to

by Della Galton.

Illustration by David McAllister.

care — not to mention being in a considerable amount of pain.

She didn't vanish, though. She didn't even frown. She laughed and her grey eyes sparkled.

"I'm sorry. I didn't mean to sound patronising. Look, why don't you let me help you? You're never going to make it back on your own. I'm Anne Granger, by the way. My father owns this lake."

Charlie frowned.

"He's not going to be very happy with me. I think this is a write-off."

49

"It's probably not beyond repair — quite," she added, narrowing her eyes thoughtfully. "If you'd like to climb over, we can tow it behind us."

He clambered into her boat, wincing as he did so.

"Are you hurt?" she asked.

"I've sprained my ankle, that's all." He held out a hand to divert her from looking.

"I'm Charlie — a proper Charlie, you could say."

But rather to his surprise she didn't laugh.

"It could happen to anyone," she said sympathetically.

Before he knew what was going on, she'd skilfully roped the boats together and had turned to face him.

"That seems painful. You are having a bad day, aren't you? Do you mind if I take a closer look at that ankle?"

"I'm a nurse," she added quickly.

He shook his head. Her fingers felt cool and expert. In any other circumstances he might have enjoyed her touch. But as it was, all he could do was watch her bowed head — she had fair hair shot through with sunshine — and wish he were somewhere else.

Mind you, if Gemma had been here, she'd have been sulking by now. Gemma was good at sulking, no matter what he did to try to please her. On good days, he suspected he got on her nerves. On bad days, he knew that Gemma would have left him already had their mothers not been such good friends.

Perhaps he should take the initiative and tell Gemma it was over. They had more bad times than good ones, now. What was the point?

I DON'T think it's broken," Anne said, finishing her examination. "But it'll be a while before you can walk on it. How were you planning on getting back to the bank if I hadn't come along?"

"I thought I could probably hop," he said, with a half smile. "My other leg's OK. I'm sorry I was churlish just now. You're right, it's been a bad day, but that was no reason to take it out on you."

"You're forgiven," she said, with a slightly wry smile. "So what do you do when you're not writing off boats and injuring yourself?"

"I teach science at Branksome Juniors. The kids are going to have a field day when I hobble in on crutches."

"That must be quite a tough job."

"I love it. I always wanted to teach. My father tried to talk me out of it. He wanted me to go into the building trade like him, but I'm not really the physical type — although I expect you'd already gathered that." It was the most he'd told anyone about himself for ages, he realised, slightly surprised.

"How about you? Was nursing a vocation for you?"

"Actually, I'm pretty boring. I followed in my parents' footsteps. Mum was a nurse and Dad was a doctor before he took early retirement and bought this business. He'd had enough of general practice and wanted to try something completely different." She paused and looked across the dark water to the line of fir trees beyond.

"I help him out when I'm not working. We've both always loved the outdoors, so this seemed like a good idea."

"Yes," he observed, realising with a pang of regret that they were almost back. It was a pity he hadn't written off her father's boat farther away from the bank!

"Do many of your customers need rescuing, then?"

"No." She grinned at him again. She had a lovely smile, bright and sparkly, like sunlight on water. "It's usually very peaceful. But it makes a nice change, to be honest."

AND then the nose of the boat was bumping against the bank. She moored up and turned to face him.

"It just so happens that I've got a pair of crutches in my car. I was taking them back to the hospital for someone who'd finished with them. If you hold on a minute, I'll get them for you."

Bang went his fantasies about her helping him out of the boat! He reminded himself that he shouldn't be having fantasies about her, anyway — he was going out with Gemma.

"Cheers," he said, when she returned with the crutches. "I really appreciate this. I'll get them back to you as soon as possible."

"There's no rush. How will you get home? Will you be all right to drive?"

"I've got an automatic," he murmured, wishing he hadn't. He'd have liked an excuse to stay around a bit longer.

"Er, about the damage." He pulled a business card from his pocket and handed it to her. "Could you ask your dad to send me the bill?"

"Don't worry. We're insured. Although I'm afraid you'll lose your deposit."

She smiled and held out her hand.

"Well, it's been nice meeting you, Charlie. I hope your ankle's better soon."

She didn't hold his hand any longer than necessary. She hadn't even glanced at his card, he thought ruefully. But then, why should she? Girls like her were never unattached. And even if she had been, she wouldn't have looked twice at an inept science teacher with wet jeans and only one working leg. He didn't blame her.

∗   ∗   ∗   ∗

True to form, Gemma found the whole thing highly amusing. Although, to be fair, that probably had something to do with the way he related the incident over the phone later that evening. Gemma might have gone off him, but she wasn't unkind.

When he saw her the following lunchtime she was quite sympathetic. He found out why over coffee.

He'd just asked for the bill when Gemma reached across and touched his hand. Unused to such spontaneous displays of affection, he glanced up and saw that her expression was serious.

"I feel terrible telling you this when you've just hurt your ankle, Charlie, but I'm afraid I've met someone else. If we're honest, we both know it hasn't been working out for a while. Don't we?"

He nodded and she rushed on.

"I'm really sorry."

"Don't be," he said, getting out some cash for the bill. "You're right, Gem, the end has been in sight for weeks."

She looked relieved. And oddly that was all he felt, too. Relief.

"Our mums won't be too happy," she observed.

"They'll get over it," he said philosophically. "They wouldn't want us to stay together just for their sake."

For some reason it was another week before it dawned on him that there was now nothing to stop him from asking Anne out for a drink.

Nothing except the fear that she'd turn him down. Or already be married with children, or engaged to a doctor, or worse, single and simply not interested in him.

So he didn't phone. He'd see her when he took the crutches back in any case. Should he go to the hospital or the boating lake? In the end he decided on the lake.

A FORTNIGHT later, he called by after work. There was no sign of Anne's car and he strolled towards the ticket hut, trying to think of how he could casually drop her name into conversation with her father.

Perhaps, with hindsight, this hadn't been such a good idea. He was hardly going to be flavour of the month.

But when he got to the hut his words dried in his throat. It wasn't Anne's father behind the counter, but Anne herself, looking even more breathtaking than he remembered.

"Well, hi," she said, smiling. "Funnily enough, I was just thinking about you."

"You were?" His heart did a triple somersault.

"Yes. I was going to ring and ask if you'd finished with those crutches. We've hit a bit of a shortage at the hospital."

"Right," he murmured, his spirits slumping. "I'll just get them for you."

There was no way he could ask her out now. The little confidence he'd had was deserting him rapidly.

52

Wroxton

WHILE strolling through the wandering lanes of this charming Oxfordshire village, you'll come across a number of thatched roofs, on houses, a tiny church — and there's even one in the middle of the pond, for the ducks!

Close to Banbury, whose cross is immortalised in the old nursery rhyme, Wroxton village grew round historical Wroxton Abbey.

J. CAMPBELL KERR.

After all, what on earth did they have in common? She was sporty and fit and capable and he couldn't even manage one outing in a rowing boat without mucking it up.

In fact, he'd already decided that he hated boats with a vengeance.

He took the crutches back to the ticket office.

"Great, thanks. I'll meet you at the back door."

He waited miserably, but when she appeared, he got the shock of his life. Her left leg was encased in plaster from ankle to knee.

"What on earth happened? Are you OK?"

"You're never going to believe this, but I was helping Dad to repair that rowing boat and I tripped over his tool box." She took the crutches from him and leaned on them.

"I wasn't as lucky as you. I fractured a bone. Dad and I have decided that boat's jinxed. Two injured ankles in the space of a fortnight. We thought we might use it for firewood."

He shook his head in amazement.

"So I won't be boating for a while," she went on softly. "I'll have to stick to dry land. It's a pity. I miss it."

"Maybe I could take you for a row on the lake," he heard himself offer. "If you trust me, that is, not to sink another boat?"

"I got the impression you weren't particularly keen on boats." She raised her eyebrows.

"I'm not the type to give up just because I didn't get it quite right the first time," he said with dignity.

"Well, in that case, yes, all right. I'm prepared to take the risk, if you are."

T HE expression in her eyes was doing all sorts of strange things to his insides.

"Life would be boring without taking the odd risk, don't you think?" he went on impulsively.

"Oh, absolutely," she agreed.

And he knew that neither of them was talking about boats any more, although there were certain similarities between boats and relationships. You started out with high hopes and, if you were really unlucky, you ended up on the rocks. If you were lucky, you ended up sailing off into the sunset.

"If you're finished for the day, maybe we could make a start now," he murmured, gazing past her towards the lake, which was beginning to turn glassy beneath the evening sky.

"You'll have to give me a minute to lock up."

He felt happier than he had for weeks, he reflected as he waited. The sun was slowly dipping below the fir trees, turning the lake into a blaze of pink and orange and gold. Sunset was fast approaching and he had a feeling he could grow to quite like boats, after all. ■

Illustration by Richard Eraut.

Learning To Fly

by Pauline Kelly.

S ARA had no idea what to buy Dad for Father's Day. Socks and scarves weren't exactly inspiring, and she had already given him a twelve-month subscription for his favourite gardening magazine for his birthday.

More pressingly, Sara had something to tell him and she wasn't finding it easy. It had been just her and Dad for five years now and since Mum had passed away, they had grown very close.

Sara had been content with her lot. Friends had left home to follow exciting careers or get married, but she had been quite happy to stay in the terraced house in the quaint old market town where she had been born to look after her father.

She had her job at the newsagent's shop in the square, attended the local history club on Monday nights and went swimming every Wednesday, she was truly at ease with what others might consider a humdrum existence.

Until she met Mark, that was.

Mark worked at the large garden centre on the outskirts of the town. She had met him last autumn when she called in on her way from the supermarket to pick up some spring bulbs for her father.

Having made her selection, Sara was having a look round the general shopping area, when her attention was caught by one of the assistants helping a couple of children to choose a gift for their mother . . .

✳   ✳   ✳   ✳

"We've saved up two whole pounds," the small girl said, proudly holding up the stash of loose change in a plastic bag.

Most of the goods on display were way beyond the children's budget, but not by a flicker did the assistant betray this fact. He indicated a stand of cut flowers.

"How about a bunch of freesias?" he suggested.

"They won't last," the boy replied. "We want something Mum can keep."

The assistant, who had dark wavy hair and a kind face, looked thoughtful.

"Does your mum have green fingers?" he asked.

"No way," the girl answered indignantly. "Our mum's hands are always very clean."

"What I meant was," he explained with a laugh, "is your mum good at growing things? That's what having green fingers is, see."

"Oh, yes. Our mum can do anything."

The assistant went to a shelf of pot plants and selected a blue campanula.

"This is a favourite of my mum's. Tell your mother she can divide it up when it outgrows the pot and plant it out in the garden. It'll go on for ever that way."

The children were delighted with their purchase and went off smiling happily.

"That's two satisfied customers," the assistant said.

Sara realised he was looking at her.

"What can I get you?" he asked. "Some winter pansies? Violas?"

Sara shook her head, her blonde, curly hair flying about her face, and indicated the bulbs in the wire basket.

"I need some fibre for these."

"The fibre's outside. I'll get you a bag."

He returned a few minutes later with a rather large bag.

"This will be quite heavy. I'll carry it to your car for you. My name's Mark. Mark Bryson."

"I'm Sara Wilks," she replied.

And so it began. Sara dropped in at the garden centre more often than usual, and Mark took to calling in at her place of work on his way home for an evening paper.

He discovered Sara's passion for orange creams and treated her to some. Then he asked her out to the cinema. Sara accepted and spent a whole week's wages on a new outfit and a cut and blow-dry at the hair stylist on the high street.

"You look good," Mark said, appreciation in his brown eyes. "I like the hair. It suits you."

The night out was a big hit and they repeated it the following weekend. After that, they met regularly. Quiet, with a shy smile and a slightly hesitant manner, Mark was a deeper thinker than Sara had first imagined. The more she saw of him the more she liked him.

By the time spring came round they were making the most of the lightening evenings, walking in the park or by the river that wound round the town, ending up in quiet little coffee shops, chatting over frothy cappuccinos.

Mark took her to his home, where she quickly felt like one of the family. Likewise, Mark became a regular caller at Sara's house and, being in the gardening trade, he and Sara's father got on splendidly.

Sara had never been happier. She had actually met someone who was like herself. Mark was proud of his home town, content to work and live there. It seemed meant. And oh, how his kisses made her bones melt.

THEN Mark dropped a bombshell.

"Remember my mate, Terry, who got married a few months back? He's come into some property with land. He and Rachel are setting up a market garden and Terry wants me to go into business with them. It's up north."

"You're leaving?" Sara stared at him, stunned. "But I thought you liked it here."

"I do, but that's not the point, is it? My present job hasn't got any prospects — but this is a great opportunity! I've talked it over with Dad and he's offered to back me. It's practically happened overnight."

His face was alight with anticipation, but Sara felt as if she had been punched in the stomach. Mark, going. And just when she had thought that everything was perfect between them.

"What a shock," she stammered. "Why didn't you mention it before?"

"I'm sorry." He bit his lip, repentant. "I was going to, but there didn't seem any point. I rejected the idea at first. I had no assets, no way of raising any money. Then Dad stepped in and . . . well, you know the rest."

There was a long silence.

"Where is this place?" Sara asked, still in shock.

"Just over the border. A village called Risley Moss."

"But, Mark, that's miles away! We'll never see each other!"

"That depends." He took her hand and held it tightly. "Sara, how about coming with me? There's a job there for you. We need someone to work in the shop." He smiled shyly, his eyes warm. "We get on great together. I've never met anyone like you before. I'd love you to be there with me. We could get married . . ."

It wasn't the proposal Sara had expected. It was too sudden, too rushed. She wanted romance, more time to get to know each other. She wanted to be wooed.

"I don't know what to say," she replied, withdrawing her hand. "There's too much involved: my job, and Dad — how would he cope on his own?"

"Just fine, I should imagine. Your dad is more capable than you give him credit for," Mark said. "You can't stay at home indefinitely and he wouldn't expect it, either. Take your time, think about it. But I have to go. Terry's at the site now, getting things started. I need to be there, too."

"So soon?" Things were getting worse. "Where will you stay?"

"There's a cottage. The place used to be a farm. Terry and Rachel are having the old farmhouse. He says it needs doing up."

Sara didn't know what else to say.

"I'm sorry. It's all happened so quickly. Sara, try to see it my way," Mark pleaded. "It's a chance to do something with my life — our lives. I have to take it."

"I see," Sara said miserably. "There's nothing more to be said then, is there?"

THAT had been back in April. It was June now and Sara still hadn't reached a decision. Neither had she spoken to Dad. His birthday had come round only a few weeks ago and she hadn't wanted to upset him. And now Father's Day loomed. Before she knew it, her own birthday would be here, and then Christmas!

She couldn't keep putting it off for ever. Mark had finished at the garden centre and was in the throes of starting his new life — he spoke of nothing else. Sometimes Sara wished it had all been a bad dream, but she knew she'd have to deal with it sooner or later.

One evening, Dad was in the garden digging up some dahlia plants for his neighbour. Ann, widowed herself, had been very supportive when Sara's mother had been taken ill and had since become a close family friend. Sara waited until her father had moved on to the greenhouse and then went to join him.

The Mad Hatters

OH, what a carry-on it is, this wedding lark, I mean,"
   Cries Hamish — he's the lucky man who's marrying
pretty Jean —
As he, and best man Charlie, try on wedding hats galore,
Enjoying harmless banter as they prance around the store.

And Mr Bell, the manager, looks on, and doesn't mind,
(Young folk must have their fun, he thinks — he's not the
   carping kind),
For, soon enough, life takes its toll, the carefree
   moments fly,
When there are little mouths to feed, and little shoes to buy.

So, "Gentlemen, may I suggest . . ." says he, with
   helpful smile.
Encouraging the two
   bright sparks to
   heed him for a
   while.
And soon our
   young men
   realise that,
   thanks to
   Mr Bell,
They've found the
   ideal suits
   and hats —
   affordable as
   well!

But . . . "Once is
   enough," hear
   Hamish cry, as
   their way home
   they wend.
"Dressing up is
   not for me!"
   "Nor me!"
   laughs his best friend.
      — *Kathleen O'Farrell.*

"Dad, I need to talk to you," she began.

He pulled out a stool from under the potting bench and indicated for her to sit.

"Thought there was something brewing. You've been awfully quiet. Is it Mark?"

"Yes," Sara replied. "Mark's going into partnership with some friends. They're starting up one of those market garden complexes where people come and buy plants and spend money in the café and shop . . ."

HE listened carefully, giving her time to explain her feelings — never easy for Sara.

"So what's the biggest issue?" he asked when she came to a stumbling stop. "Is it the fact that Mark went ahead with his plans, regardless of what you wanted? Or is it the thought of change?"

Sara frowned at him.

"What do you mean?"

"Sara, when your mother and I were newly married an elderly lady called Mrs Bates lived next door where Ann is now. She was full of home-spun philosophies." He smiled. "When you were born, Mrs Bates said that parents had to give their children two important qualities — roots and wings.

"We thought it was funny at the time, but what she meant was quite profound. You make sure that your children have all the love and security they need while they're growing up. And when they're ready, you let them go."

Sara's frown deepened.

"But I never wanted to go," she said.

"Exactly. Perhaps your mother and I made your roots too deep. All I know, Sara, is that, in your shoes, I wouldn't hesitate. I'd have followed your mum to the ends of the earth to be with her."

"You sound as if you want rid of me!" Sara gave a shrug. "But it's you I'm most bothered about. Who'd look after everything if I wasn't here to do it?"

"I would! I'm not completely helpless, you know. But I don't want to be the cause of holding you back." Her father smiled kindly. "But of course I'd miss you, and no doubt the house wouldn't be as spotless as it is now, but so what? Nothing would give me more pleasure than to see you happily settled. I like Mark. He's a good man."

"I know."

"So what's the problem? Don't you love him?"

"Oh, I do, it's just . . ."

". . . a little romance would have helped?" Her father smiled. "My guess is that Mark must have a lot on his plate at the moment. I should go with him and see this place."

"But that's the point. Mark hasn't asked me to go and see it again. Knowing him, he's waiting to see what I want to do."

"Well, then, ask him about it again! It can't hurt, can it?" her dad said to her with a wide grin.

"I suppose not," Sara replied with a sigh.

Next morning, Mark called at the shop on his way up north and told her he wouldn't be seeing her till the weekend, when he was due home again. Sara said nothing about him taking her to see the place. He looked so excited, she could feel he was already beginning to drift away from her.

"I'll ring you," he said, before giving her a farewell kiss.

Sara watched as he opened the door to the shop and, sending her a wink, was gone.

With that, she put her mind to the morning rush, working as if on automatic, her heart heavy. She told herself she was making too much of the situation. Mark had every right to go ahead with a career, and Dad had been more generous and broad-thinking than she could have imagined. Why, then, was she left with this feeling of hurt?

*   *   *   *

True to his word, Mark rang that evening to tell Sara of all his news. The formalities were being drawn up and he was full of plans.

Sara listened as he spoke eagerly of seed beds and polytunnels. They were aiming to supply the flower trade, he said. Florist shops and floral art enthusiasts were enjoying a boom at the moment. Terry's Rachel was into all that in a big way. But never once did he mention Sara's part in the proceedings.

"What are you doing tonight?" Mark asked suddenly.

"Well, it's Monday, so I might go along to the History Club," Sara replied. "I haven't been back for ages."

"That's what comes of getting mixed up with the guy from the garden centre!" Mark's chuckle rippled over the line. "Better press on. I'll speak to you tomorrow. Cheers, Sara."

No "love you lots" or "miss you", Sara observed, replacing the receiver. She might as well have been one of the lads for all the special attention he paid her!

For the rest of the week, Sara kept busy, trying not to give herself space to dwell on how it had been when Mark was there. Even so, the week crawled by and she couldn't wait for the weekend, when he would be home again.

Saturday came at last and every time the shop door opened, Sara's heart leapt in anticipation. But it was never Mark. When lunchtime arrived and he still hadn't turned up she rang him on his mobile.

"Hi, Sara." He sounded surprised. "I've been meaning to call you. Look, something cropped up. I won't be able to make it this weekend after all. You know how it is."

Sara's hopes crashed.

"Oh, yes, I know," she muttered before she could stop herself. "I know that

I come second to a load of pot plants and . . . and strawberries!"

"Say that again?"

"Come on — it's obvious. Gardening matters more to you than anything else."

"Sara, you're brilliant!" Mark gasped. "You've just hit on the perfect solution to our problem! There's masses of land here, more than we know what to do with. We could plant it up with soft fruit bushes. I can see the sign now, *pick your own gooseberries and blackcurrants*. We could even plant an apple orchard . . ."

"Oh, so I do have my uses," Sara said wryly.

"Of course you do." He rambled on with huge enthusiasm and Sara sighed.

It was no good. When Mark was in work mode — and that was most of the time — she might as well be on the other side of the moon.

"Mark," she said. "I've got to go. Are you sure you're not coming home?"

"Positive. Sorry."

He didn't sound it, though, and Sara's spirits fell even further.

"See you next weekend," he said, ringing off.

Famous last words, she thought to herself.

THE following week limped by, highlighted by calls from Mark. They'd invested in a work vehicle, he said. He'd be driving down on Sunday. Noting the weekend had now dwindled to a single day, Sara didn't raise her hopes too much. A late call on Saturday, however, made her feel better.

"Thought we'd go for a spin tomorrow. I'll call for you. About seven?"

"Seven?" Sara repeated in shock.

"I know it's a little early, but I need to pick up some things from the agricultural merchants off the bypass."

Sara bit back a sigh. She might have known there would be an ulterior motive. They chatted some more and then rang off.

Next morning she dressed carefully in pale pink cropped trousers and a cotton top, tied back her hair loosely, and was ready when the pick-up drew up outside. She slipped out quietly so as not to waken Dad.

Mark greeted her with a kiss.

"Hi. What a sight for sore eyes! Hope you don't get those things mucky."

"Why?" Sara asked. "Where are we heading?"

"Mystery tour." He started the engine. "Let's get the suppliers over with. Then the day is ours."

They wound their way through the silent early morning streets and were soon pulling in at the agricultural merchants on the ring road. As well as the usual farming tackle it also stocked garden equipment. Into the truck went sections of rustic trellis and some fencing posts.

"What's that for?" Sara asked curiously.

"Display purposes," Mark said, securing the load with a rope. "Right. Let's

Crail

SITUATED at one end of Fife's East Neuk, Crail Harbour was an important mediaeval trading port for Europe — hence the distinctive red roof tiles, brought over from the Low Countries as ballast. The ancient and charming little town has always been a magnet to those who enjoy the peace and tranquillity it offers.

J. CAMPBELL KERR

make a move!"

They set off, avoiding the busier routes, keeping to leafy by-roads, pressing onwards until Sara was sure they must be lost. Mark, however, seemed to know exactly where he was going.

Sara stole a glance at his profile. He looked sun-browned and fit and somehow older. She noticed the firm set of his chin and the fact that his hair needed cutting, and blushed when he caught her eye and gave her a wink.

"Almost there. Risley Moss, here we come."

"This is it?" Sara cried. "Why didn't you say we were heading here?"

"I told you — it's a surprise. It's not that small — more of a town really. The market garden is on the other side."

They drove through the village, slowing down at the entrance to a cobbled yard. Mark gave her another glance, an apprehensive one this time.

"Here we are. It's still a bit of a tip yet, but we're getting there."

THEY pulled into a derelict-looking farmyard with barns and outbuildings and a large house. At one side, the town encroached; at the other, the fields were marked out with coloured tape. Terry was turning over the neglected ground with a small tractor and plough.

Mark jumped out of the pick-up and went to open the passenger door.

"This way."

He took her hand, leading her past a building that was to be turned into a shop with restaurant, leaving the yard and going on to where the gardens of a housing development backed on to the straggling boundary hedge. Mark stopped in front of a small dwelling solidly built of dark old brick.

"This is the cottage."

He pushed open the stout front door and stood aside for Sara to enter.

"Oh!" she gasped, glancing round in surprise. A great deal of work had been done. The woodwork was stripped to the original pitch pine, the walls were colour-washed and, she saw, going through to the back, what promised to be a very pleasant kitchen was in the process of being fitted.

"The garden's a mess," Mark said, glancing through the window that was smudged with paint. "I haven't had time to tackle it yet. That's what the fencing is for. I thought you might like to grow roses up it . . ."

"You mean," Sara said, "that this is what you've been up to? This is why you couldn't get back last weekend?"

"That's about it. The place wasn't in very good shape. I wanted to bring you out here at the start but I couldn't let you see it as it was. You'd have run a mile! It's been all go, what with the market garden to sort out and this wreck of a house to lick into shape."

"Oh, Mark!" She put her arms around him and hugged him. "And I thought . . . oh, never mind. I was wrong. I should have trusted you. I might have known you'd have something up your sleeve!"

"So you like it?" he said, holding her close. "We can change the colours if you want."

"No, it's perfect as it is."

"Sara, I wanted to show you how much I think of you. I'm not much good at saying how I feel but I do love you very much. Please say you'll marry me."

"I will. Of course I will. There's nothing I want more," Sara gasped.

They kissed, and then stood there in their home-to-be, clasped closely, lost in the magic of the moment.

Mark was the first to break away.

"I was panicking in case you wouldn't want to leave your dad. We're not all that far away. He can come and stay any time. We can go back later and fetch him if you'd like. I'm sure he'd love to have a look round."

"Yes, he would. I was wrong. I was genuinely concerned for Dad, but he insisted I shouldn't be. He said other things, too. I was miffed at the time." And then, horrifyingly, something struck her.

"Mark, it's Father's Day and I haven't got Dad anything! I couldn't think what to buy and kept putting it off. He'll have his card and no gift — and I always buy him something!"

"There's no problem," Mark said reassuringly. "We'll have a word with Rachel. She makes garden ornaments amongst other things. She's got loads of ideas for the shop — and I'm sure you and she will get on brilliantly. Rachel's sure to have some memento you can give him. Besides —"

"Go on." So much had happened that Sara's head was spinning.

"I reckon once your dad hears our news it'll be celebrations all round. It'll make this a Father's Day to remember."

And it was! ■

Lost And Found

FLOSS stared down at the long grass. The man had definitely dropped his wallet. She thought she'd seen something fall as he climbed into the taxi, but she wasn't sure. Perhaps she should have called out, but it didn't feel respectful. Young ladies in Rwanda shouldn't draw attention to themselves in that way.

She bent down to pick up the wallet. It was fat — there must be many Rwandan francs inside. She looked around, but the street was deserted. There wasn't even a hotel in the area. The man must have been walking along the road-side and, seeing the taxi, hailed it and climbed in. Its rear lights had already been swallowed up by the night.

What could she do? How could she return the wallet to its owner? She couldn't just leave it here on the grass verge. Anyone might take it. One of her grandmother's famous sayings came to mind.

"If the palm of the hand itches, it signifies the coming of great wealth."

Was her palm itchy? Floss didn't think so, and why should it be? The money wasn't hers. She slipped the wallet into her handbag, and continued her long walk home.

Her day had been difficult. She had walked into the centre of Remara from her mother's small *adobe* in the vain hope of finding some extra work. Her friend, Aggie, had said she'd heard they were taking on staff at the Airport View restaurant and bar, but after Floss had spent two long hours waiting for Mr Gatwato, the owner, things hadn't looked very promising.

"I have a diploma from the Hosanna Tailoring and Business School," Floss told him. "I can do books and I have management skills. I would like to work for you, and I would be an asset to your business."

MR GATWATO looked surprised.

"Why would I need a sewing girl? Why are you here?"

"My friend, Aggie, told me you are looking for people to wait on tables," Floss explained.

"And if I give you work," Mr Gatwato said, his eyes narrowing, "you will stay only long enough to find sewing work elsewhere, and then you will leave."

Floss avoided his gaze. What could she say? It was perfectly true. Her plan had been to work just long enough to save 50,000 Rwandan francs. That would be enough to set herself up with a stall at the local market, thirty pieces of Batik, a sewing machine and a filled iron with enough charcoal to keep it hot. She had already saved 35,000 francs and ordered a sewing machine, but she still

66

by Pam
Weaver.

Illustration by
Maggie Palmer.

needed to find the rest of the money if her dream was to become a reality.

Mr Gatwato shook his head.

"I can see by your face that this is the case," he said, and he walked away from her, dismissing her with a wave of his hand. "I have no need for sewing girls."

Disappointed, Floss couldn't bear to return home empty handed. She thought of another of her grandmother's sayings.

"Unless you call out, who will open the door?"

She had to keep going. She'd been foolish enough to boast earlier to her sisters that she would easily find work. So Floss spent the rest of the afternoon looking for an opening.

But it was hopeless. The hot, dusty streets were crowded with people. Floss enquired in almost every shop, but it seemed that nobody was hiring today.

By four o'clock she was tired. She found a shop selling sodas, lifted the net curtain hanging over the doorway and stepped inside. With her last remaining coins she ordered an orange drink and, as she sipped it, considered her options.

Life wasn't easy. Her father and brother had been tragically killed more than ten years ago. Since then, her mother and grandmother had kept the family together, eking out a living selling second-hand clothing in the market, but it had been a struggle.

Floss loved her mother, but shared a special bond with her grandmother. Although she was old and not as nimble as she used to be, Floss still hung on her every word. She was a mine of information and very respected in the community. Her sayings were famous. In fact, it was said that Floss's grandmother had a Rwandese proverb for every occasion. But just lately, she'd changed, it seemed. Somehow, she'd lost her sparkle.

Floss sighed. She and her sisters were luckier than most. They never went to bed hungry, but sometimes they did go without shoes. Sometimes they had to stay at home because their mother didn't have their school fees.

"Let me stop my schooling," Floss once suggested to her mother and grandmother. "Then you can pay for Henrietta and Rick, and I can work with you on the market."

But her mother wouldn't hear of it, and nor would her grandmother.

"If you educate a man, you educate an individual. If you educate a woman, you educate a family," her grandmother said.

After that, Floss made it her top priority to do well. There was a time when it looked as if she would be forced to give up near to her final exams but, fortunately, the pastor of their local church had agreed that the fellowship would pay for her last remaining term. This spurred her on further and she passed her exams with flying colours.

The money for her to attend the Hosanna Tailoring and Business School came from people living abroad, who sent money to sponsor children.

All these helping hands had made Floss determined to succeed. She also felt a great deal of responsibility to do so. A sewing business would give her a degree of independence, too, which would always mean a steady income for the family, no matter what.

Unlike her wise grandmother, most people said it was a waste of money educating girls.

"Girls only got married and then their husbands would support them," they said. Indeed, that prophecy seemed to be coming true, even for Floss.

Kagame Emmanuel wanted her to marry him and, although she had agreed, sometimes she wasn't sure she'd done the right thing. He had a good job in construction, and in modern-day Rwanda there was plenty of work to do. As long as he kept away from his banana beer-drinking friends, he'd do well . . .

"You should hurry up and marry a good-looking man like that," her friends told her time and again. "Most girls would jump at the chance!"

Her grandmother was a little more cautious, though.

"The teeth are smiling," she said, "but is the heart?"

"Don't you trust him?" Floss asked anxiously.

"I asked the question," her grandmother replied. "It's up to you to find the answer."

BACK home, the family and Kagame had gathered for their meal of fried mashed banana, rice, cassava leaves and a little broth.

"When do you start work?" her sister Henrietta asked, almost as soon as Floss walked through the door.

"Mr Gatwato didn't need anyone else."

"But Aggie said . . ."

"Aggie was wrong.

"Grandmother, don't you always say, 'What is bad luck for one man is good luck for another'?" Floss said as she drew out the wallet and laid it down beside their one and only candle.

Her mother gasped as she undid the button and opened it out. It was stuffed with money.

"There must be a million francs there," Kagame said, his eyes lighting up.

"We're rich!" Rick cried.

Floss took everything out. A credit card — no, four; a photograph of a white woman with two small children and five hundred British pounds. Floss did a quick calculation, and worked out that the money was worth roughly five hundred thousand Rwandan franks. There was also a small card.

Ethan Dewey, 56 Mortlake Road, Hove, and a mobile phone number were printed on it.

"It belongs to that man," she said.

"But nobody saw you pick it up?" Henrietta asked.

Floss shook her head.

"Then keep it!" Henrietta's words hung in the air.

Floss jerked her head up to find everyone looking at her.

"Who's to know?" Kagame said with a shrug of his shoulders. "He's very rich. He must be rich to come all the way to Rwanda. He can afford to lose this money."

"Kagame is right," Henrietta reasoned. "People from the West donate money to help us — you yourself went to the Hosanna Tailoring and Business School with money from sponsors."

Rick nodded.

"All Westerners are very rich," he said.

Floss's heart was beating fast, and she glanced at her grandmother. It was all very tempting. If she were to look for this man, she would also have to find the money to make a mobile call.

"The ruin of a nation begins in the homes of its people," her grandmother murmured.

"And you are a foolish old woman," Kagame teased. "Nobody saw it happen except Floss. Where's the harm?"

Her grandmother turned away and, after that, nothing more was said.

"Keep the money and we could get married very soon," Kagame cooed in Floss's ear later, as he left.

BUT that night, Floss lay on her pallet listening to the crickets outside. Her mind was in a whirl.

They were right, her siblings and Kagame — who would know? She'd be a fool to turn down this fantastic opportunity. That money could set the whole family up for life.

Her siblings need never fear they'd have to give up their schooling because they didn't have the fees . . . Floss herself could start her business, not in the market and open to all weathers; with this money she could afford to rent a little lock-up shop of her own.

And Kagame had grand plans, too. After the wedding, he said, he would be able to make a start on a brick villa instead of an *adobe*. So little money to this Englishman was a life-changing fortune to them.

On the other hand, maybe the man wasn't so rich after all. Maybe that was all the money he had. Her grandmother, normally so vocal in her opinions and sayings, had been very quiet all evening. Did her silence mean that she agreed with the rest of the family?

The moon rose and Floss watched the stars through the open window. She fell into a troubled sleep, wondering what she should do.

The wallet was still in her handbag when she and her mother set off for the market the following morning. Her grandmother was staying at home to do the washing.

Their stall was deep inside the covered area. That meant they were at a disadvantage, because people only came in if they particularly wanted second-hand clothing, or if it was raining.

Although Floss and her mother rarely had browsers, they did have a

Castleton

LIKE many attractions in Derbyshire, Castleton has a nickname, which is "Gem of the Peaks". Lying at the end of the charmingly named Hope Valley, the compact village centre is crammed with interesting shops and many a pleasant hour can be spent wandering through the back streets.

This delightful scene shows Waterside, a lovely walk along by the river.

J. CAMPBELL KERR.

reputation for good quality clothing which was always spotlessly clean.

Today was a good day. By the time they reached the market, it was raining. Henrietta and Rick weren't too happy that they would get wet on their way to school, and their grandmother would struggle to dry the washing, but it meant the market was particularly crowded.

Floss and her mother worked hard all the morning and made plenty of good sales.

By lunchtime, the rain had stopped and Floss decided to take a walk.

"I may be a while," she told her mother. "I want to see Kagame."

Her mother smiled.

"Pop back home to see your grandmother, too," she said. "I'm worried about her — she's not seemed herself just lately."

Floss nodded and looked under the tablecloth for her handbag. She felt her heart sink as she looked around the bottom of the stall and discovered it was missing. Her mother was busy with a customer. Floss searched frantically. Who could have moved it? Her mother? A thief?

"What are you looking for?" her mother asked as the customer left.

"My bag." Floss couldn't hide the anxiety in her voice.

Her mother delved around the back under one of the boxes.

"I put it here for safe keeping."

A wave of relief swept over Floss as she thought of all the money it contained.

KAGAME wasn't at the construction site. The foreman said he had sent his little brother to say he was sick. A sudden illness, apparently. Floss was surprised.

"But he was very well last night," she blurted out, immediately regretting her outburst. The foreman looked very annoyed, and she hoped she hadn't lost Kagame his job.

Her grandmother was busy draping the washing over the bushes which surrounded their *adobe*. Floss walked up and hugged her. When she stepped back, she saw tears in the old woman's eyes.

"What, Mma? What is it?"

"I shall miss you, child, when you marry."

"We shall come and see you often."

Her grandmother shook her head.

"You will not have time for a foolish old woman."

"Mma, I owe you so much. Of course I shall come back to see you!"

"You may think so now," she said, "but that Kagame — already he has changed you. He has taken away your spirit."

Floss laughed.

"Please don't worry. I haven't changed, and I shall always be your little child. Don't worry."

Kagame was with his friends in the bar. He was also a little drunk. He had his arm around a young woman, but when Floss put her head around the door, he came outside straight away to meet her.

"I was celebrating," he protested when he saw the gentle rebuke in her eyes.

"Celebrating?"

"Our marriage," he told her, nuzzling her neck. "Our special good fortune."

"Who is that girl?"

"She's nobody." He laughed dismissively. "I may look at other girls, but I always come running back to you, Floss."

"I need you to take me to the Hotel Englise," she said.

E was slightly shorter than she remembered. Pale-faced and wearing a floppy hat, white shirt, shorts and long grey socks with sandals, he stood outside the Hotel Englise, anxiously looking up and down the road.

Kagame drove past the entrance and pulled up.

"Why do you want to come here?"

"I am returning the wallet," she told him calmly.

"You must be mad," he snapped. "Why? No-one would have known!"

"I would have known," she said.

"If I had known that's what you wanted," he said. "I would have refused to bring you."

"I know," she said quietly, and climbed out of the car.

She stared back at him, noticing for the first time the hardness in his eyes. He was controlling his feelings, but he was furious.

"Go on, then," he snapped. "And make sure you get a reward."

Floss walked up to the pale foreigner.

"Mr De-way?" she asked shyly. "I rang you on your mobile."

"Dewey," he corrected. They both hesitated. "Five Mortlake Road, Hove," he added.

She handed him the wallet and he checked the contents.

"It's all there," she cried, suddenly concerned that he might accuse her of taking something.

He nodded.

"Yes, it is." His tone was softer, less tense. "Thank you."

He turned to leave. As she stood in the road, her eyes smarting with disappointment, she heard Kagame open the car door.

"Ask him," he shouted in the Kinyardwandan language. "Make him give you a reward, you stupid woman!"

Even as the words left his lips, Floss knew she would never marry Kagame. Her grandmother always said a test brings out a quality in a person, and right now, she saw something in Kagame that she didn't like at all.

The man mounted the steps and went back into the hotel. Kagame cursed aloud and slammed the car door. Floss turned to see him roaring off up the road.

So much for honesty! She sighed. She had done the right thing, and yet she had lost her fiancé. She had also lost her lift, and this place was easily five kilometres from her home. Now she was going to have a very long walk.

But she wasn't sorry. She felt better than she had done the whole time she'd had the wallet in her handbag.

"Just a minute." A woman had appeared at the top of the steps and called after her in her native tongue.

Floss turned back to see the very smartly-dressed lady running down the steps towards her. The man reappeared at the top, the wallet still in his hand.

"It's all there," Floss protested again. "I didn't touch any of it."

"Where do you work?" the lady asked.

"I don't have work of my own," Floss replied hesitantly. What had this to do with the wallet?

"So you do nothing," she said. "Are you lazy?"

"No, no!" Floss cried horrified. "I help my mother in the market on her stall, and I have a diploma from the Hosanna Tailoring and Business School. One day, I shall have my own business."

"Excellent!" the lady exclaimed. "I was going to offer you a job as a chambermaid, but now that I know you have a qualification, I must tell you I need a receptionist. If your references are good, are you willing to train?"

Floss was conscious of her mouth opening and shutting, but no sound came out.

"But . . . I don't understand," she said eventually.

"It's quite simple," the lady replied. "When this gentleman lost his wallet, I told him this would be the last he saw of it. I said if anyone handed it in, I would eat my hat."

Floss's eyes widened.

"I have no hat!" The lady laughed. "But I would be pleased to have someone like you working for me."

I COULD not believe my ears," Floss said when she told her family about the job, later that night.

Her mother and siblings were thrilled. Everyone agreed that a good steady job with prospects was a million times better than the money in the wallet.

"What will you do with the sewing machine when it comes?" Henrietta asked.

"If I cannot learn the job, I shall do my sewing."

"You will learn," her mother said.

"Do you think you will miss Kagame?" Rick asked.

Floss didn't have to think about that. She shook her head vigorously and laughed. It felt like a weight had gone from her shoulders.

She glanced at her grandmother. For once, the old lady said nothing, but Floss couldn't help noticing that the old sparkle was back in her eyes. ∎

Count Your Blessings...

THE hut *again*!" I said disdainfully, disappointment clearly telling in my voice. "I'd thought that this summer, what with the kids off doing their own thing, we could at least try something different, be a bit daring or exotic for once."

The trouble was, my husband was getting used to my moans of late. We'd been in a bit of a rut and he seemed happy staying there. My feelings just didn't seem to count any more, and that was what really hurt . . .

I sighed and returned to the last chapter of my book, which took me off to a better place — a romantic, exciting world where dreams came true and happiness stayed for ever.

All that seems a long time ago, because Dave got his way as usual, and for the umpteenth year we've come down here to our little bungalow on the shiny Dorset coast.

by May Canner.

It was no more than a beach hut, really, but big enough to sleep the family, and the scene of many happy holidays.

Perhaps that was the trouble; this year we'd be alone and I didn't know if I was ready for that.

We'd inherited the hut from my gran. She and Gramps had bought it years ago when they were built for people who couldn't afford expensive holidays abroad.

All the family have used the hut over the years, and some close friends, too, because it seemed a shame to leave it unoccupied for a lot of the season — much better to share the happiness around, I'd thought. There's hardly a week goes by, right from early June until the schools go back in September, that it isn't full of love and laughter, just like Gran and Gramps would have wanted.

Now, of course, these huts cost a fortune and many of our holiday neighbours own expensive toys like jet-skis and boats. But somehow that seems rather sad to me . . .

*   *   *   *

We arrive on a hot thundery afternoon after a stuffy journey along the motorway that had taken hours more than it should have. Why Dave chose a bank holiday weekend to start our journey, I'll never know!

We park in the carpark at Hengistbury Head and take the little noddy-train ride to our beach-fronted palace, so aptly named *Travellers' Rest*.

I used to love coming here when the children were young, but this year is different. It looks very much to me as if all the happy times have gone for ever and there's nothing I can do about it.

Todd, our eldest, has gone off to Greece with his mates and goodness knows what mayhem he's up to! Dave says I shouldn't think about it and that he's a sensible lad and, of course, he's right.

Mia, our daughter, just turned seventeen, has gone to Spain with her best friend, Kelly, and her family. I'm not sure if I like the new-found freedom and togetherness that comes when your children finally fly the nest.

After all, what will we talk about? What will we do here without the children? It's been bad enough at home just recently since they've gone off to college and university and sometimes all we seem to do is bicker.

AS I push open the doors of the hut a million memories greet us like old friends. Buckets and spades hang from a hook on the wall; various familiar beach toys, added to each year, sit in a box on the floor waiting for the fun to begin.

And there, pinned to the cupboards, are photographs of every holiday that we've ever spent here for the last twenty years or so, including some of my sister, Jackie, and her brood taken only three weeks ago and all of them looking so happy.

They've left a note wishing us a happy holiday and telling us all they got up to. Memories from the past in black-and-white photos sit alongside more recent times. Snaps of my gran and gramps, mum and dad, and me as a child on happy family holidays, a lifetime ago, now just a faint smile on the face of time.

I feel tired and jaded and it isn't down to the long journey, either. It's down to life, or rather the passing of time.

The sounds and smells here are the same as always — of seaweed, sun-cream and summer. There's an air of expectation flying about the place as families arrive pale and tired from the cities, then depart for home again, bronzed and relaxed after their holiday break. There are some familiar faces and some new ones, too.

But I feel lost here this year, and wish we hadn't come. Misery floods me. Why on earth do I feel like this?

"Right!" Dave's exclamation makes me jump. "I'll go down to the café and get us a snack whilst you unpack. Then I thought we could get the ferry across the run and have a drink in the pub later. Maybe some supper, too? I seem to remember they do a mean fisherman's pie there. How does that sound?"

D AVE, no doubt sensing my mood, tries to jolly me along.
I stare at him. He looks so happy and excited, like he always does when we come here. I force a smile and feel guilty at my moodiness and negativity. I don't want to feel like this, I think with a heavy sigh.

"Just fine, love," I say, forcing brightness into my voice. "I'll have a tuna bap, please."

I smile, trying to cheer myself up.

"That's more like it, Kath!" Dave beams. "I'll be catching fresh fish for you from tomorrow onwards. I thought I'd do that fishing trip that Todd and I took last year. Then I may do some night fishing off the beach later in the week. Won't be long, love . . ."

He's gone and I'm left fuming.

A fishing trip! Tomorrow! Our first day here and he's off on his own and planning more trips for the rest of the week by the sound of it. I sigh even louder than before.

It hasn't been a very good six months for us. We seem to be drifting apart like the little boats that bob at the water's edge outside, pulling in different directions. Our relationship feels shipwrecked.

I look out on all the happiness and feel none. All this place does for me this year is highlight all the storms that are my life at present.

I wipe down the kitchen surfaces and put the kettle on, making a determined effort to be more positive. Perhaps a cup of tea will make me feel better — or a magnum of champagne and a tropical paradise with Tom

Cruise in attendance!

Yes, that would do it, I think, as I put the tea bags in two mugs that are as old as I am.

"Sorry, love, they were out of tuna! Eggy ones OK?"

Dave's cheerful voice interrupts my daydream.

"I got some crisps, too . . ."

I hate eggs, but I eat them just the same. I don't want to create any more tension, especially not today and especially not here.

I unpack whilst he sits and takes in the remainder of the warm afternoon sunshine. The storm still rumbles somewhere out at sea.

Then, later, we take the ferry across to the other side of the run and the pub. The sun is sinking fast, melting into the sea from its home in a beautiful mackerel grey-blue sky. This place has a magic about it no matter how hard I try to ignore it.

"Look, love." Dave points to a sign on the jetty.

Fishing trips. Bait and rods supplied. Meet here eight o'clock by The Rosie.

The "Friend" Remembers Wartime Chanteuses & Entertainers

Ivy Benson 1913 — 1993

IVY BENSON, the talented musician and bandleader, is remembered with great affection by her many fans.

Ivy was born in Leeds and, from an early age, a career in music was inevitable. Her father played with the Leeds Symphony Orchestra and in the pit of the Leeds Empire, and intended his daughter to become a concert pianist. Ivy therefore took piano lessons from the age of three, and it was only later that she learned to play the clarinet, saxophone and trombone.

Ivy's first job was in a shoe shop, followed by a factory, but she added to her wages by playing in bands such as Edna Croudfoot's Rhythm Girls in the evenings.

It became an ambition of Ivy's to lead a girls' band that could really play well, and she formed her twenty-piece band in 1940.

The band had its first break when it gained a contract with the Mecca Ballroom in Manchester. Shortly after this, in 1943, the band got its first radio engagement on the BBC. Many male bandleaders decided to protest and put round a petition against the band in an attempt to halt the broadcast.

Despite this, however, Ivy Benson's All-Girls' Band went from strength to strength. They were one of the troops' favourites during the war, receiving fan letters from many servicemen — they were even the first band to play in Berlin after its liberation.

Ivy therefore succeeded in her ambition to lead a real band and, for the first time, an all-girl band was taken seriously. Some five hundred girls passed

"That'll do me nicely," he says with a smile.

I feel myself bristle.

"What are you going to do tomorrow?" he asks airily. "Have a trip into town? Or a lazy day on the beach, sunning yourself?"

78

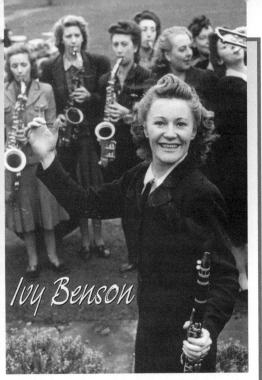

Ivy Benson

under Ivy's wing over the years — all of whom she trained herself. Despite a lack of female players to choose from in the early days, Ivy always managed to get the best out of her girls. She was even known to put down her baton and play along with the band.

After the big band era came to an end, Ivy kept on playing with her band at civic dances and balls. In the early Eighties she moved to Clacton-on-Sea and, at the age of seventy-three, she went solo, swapping her saxophone for an electric organ and entertaining folks at venues along the sea-front.

Once dubbed "the godmother of Britain's girl pop stars", she kept up her musical links until her death.

I'm so furious I can't answer. Is he really this unfeeling and selfish, I ask myself. Or is it me?

We sit outside the pub and I drink a glass of wine, finding my mood improves along with the setting sun. My husband looks so handsome here in the sunset that my heart flutters a little. He hasn't changed all that much over the years, and I know he loves me.

I love him, too, but it's like I've become a bit invisible, or at least that's how it feels to me sometimes . . .

"Weather set fair for the morning," he says, sounding all nautical. "Mackerel for tea, I shouldn't wonder, or a straying tuna if you're lucky!"

"Well, if you gut them, I'll cook them!" I joke and he puts his arm around me and kisses me soundly. For the first time since we arrived — actually, for the first time in a long while, I feel happy and relaxed.

I WAKE to the raucous cry of gulls and automatically reach out in the cosiness of our little bed but I'm alone. Looking at my watch, I see it's nearly nine and Dave has already left to do battle with the giant mackerel.

I've a bit of a headache, and outside the sun makes me squint in the brightness of the day.

I walk down to the ferry, the fine white sand hot between my toes. Everywhere are children, and how I miss mine! I don't think you realise when they're small how quickly the passage of time will change things.

A MAN and a little boy stand at the water's edge. The child has curly, sun-bleached hair framing a cherub-like face. I think he must be the man's grandson; the love and familiarity between them is palpable. He's a beautiful child with eyes bluer than the sea. He rubs sand between tiny chubby fingers, and squeals with delight as it falls back into the water, looking so like Todd at two or three.

His little trunks are weighted down with wet sand as he constantly battles to rescue them against gravity. He makes me smile, but close by, my tears wait. I push them back, determined not to cry on such a beautiful morning.

The boy's grandpa smiles at me with empathy. I suppose he remembers what it was like, that lonely gap between children and grandchildren.

Farther along the beach I see a little girl with curly sandy-red hair, so like my daughter Mia at that age, with her skinny little legs. She's like a dainty water sprite, dancing in the gentle surf, giggling and running to escape the incoming waves, which must seem like huge breakers to this little fairy of a girl.

She shrieks and runs backwards, her hand reaching out for the reassuring closeness of her mother.

Now, underneath my glasses, a tear finally escapes and so do I — into the anonymous queue for the ferry.

I sit and have coffee at the café on the run. I have a coffee and Danish. I'm spoiling myself today. Then I watch the jet-skiers ride the waves and the boats head out to sea, gingerly manoeuvring through the narrow channel of the run.

Greedy seagulls squabble for ragged scraps hanging from last-night's discarded lobster pots that adorn the walkway.

This place has a special magic all of its own and — at last — I feel glad that we came. I want to tell Dave that I'm sorry, that he's welcome to his fishing trip. I want him to enjoy it; he works so hard for us all.

I sit and reflect on what exactly has been wrong between us and, in one of those moments of clarity, I see that it's me who's the problem, who *has* been the problem, all along. It's not the holiday destination, or Dave. I've reached a time in my life where everything seems to be changing, including me, and if I'm honest, it makes me feel a little redundant.

I promise myself I'll make it up to him. We'll have a brilliant holiday and I'll leave happy photographs for my cousin, Sheila, who'll be the last visitor here this summer.

I'm *glad* my children are healthy and independent, venturing out into the world! They have the whole planet to explore, a life to live, and there will be other times here at the hut, probably with their children, our grandchildren, all of us together again . . .

But for now, for a little break in time, it's just us two, and now I realise that can be just as rewarding.

I buy a book that takes my fancy from the stand, a huge bar of chocolate and a trendy new sun-hat. Then I head back to the hut for a day of pure relaxation and indulgence. I smile ruefully when I recall that this was something I used to dream about when our kids were small and demanding all of my time.

The book is riveting and soon I lose myself as I read about Sienna and her hard life as the wife of a Cornish fisherman. She lives in a time fraught with danger, insecurity and devastating poverty. I read about love, life, and death and the unimaginable hardship of times gone by.

I make a tuna roll for lunch and, in the gentle July afternoon, eat my chocolate and drink my tea, savouring this new feeling of tranquillity.

I watch tired mums look on enviously, as they struggle to get tired, over-excited children ready for supper and bed. I see elderly couples walk barefoot, hand in hand along the water's edge, glad to be together for yet another summer at this idyllic place.

Now the sun is sinking fast. I shower, change and make myself glamorous for that man of mine.

I LOOK at my watch. It's getting late. I can't remember now what time *The Rosie* was due back, but it's gone eight and I'm almost sure he should be here by now. I feel suddenly uneasy. I put on my flip-flops and start the five-minute walk to the ferry. I'm aware my heart is beating faster than normal and I have that feeling in the pit of my stomach, like when you lose sight of your child for a few moments in a supermarket.

I board the ferry and it takes only a couple of minutes to cross the run. Already I can see a huddle of people standing where *The Rosie* is normally moored. I push to get off the boat and find myself almost running the hundred yards or so to where the people are congregating.

Voices now, with an anxious edge to them.

She was due back an hour ago. Has anyone called the coastguard . . .?

I catch my breath and turn to a man who looks local and weatherbeaten, like an old fisherman.

"Is there something wrong? My husband's out on the boat."

I'm alarmed by the shrug of his shoulders and the look in his eyes. Why can't he reassure me?

My heart's pounding now and my mouth is dry, but then . . . a little cheer goes up, and there, chugging smokily and noisily along the run comes *The Rosie*, home at last. And there, waving, is my husband, tanned and happy, triumphantly holding up his catch of mackerel and beaming from ear to ear.

Just for a second I think of Sienna and her children and a hard life in hard times, and I'm so grateful, so very grateful for my happy life . . .

When Dave jumps on to the quayside, I fall into his arms and all those tears I've just about held on to for weeks spill out, releasing me, setting free all my fears and insecurities to float away on the fast evening tide.

"I love you so much . . ." I sob as I cling to him.

"I love you, too, Kath." After a tight hug, he holds me at arm's length.

"What's wrong, love?" he asks gently, but I shake my head and smile through my tears, squeezing his hands as he starts to explain.

"We had some engine trouble just as we set off for home. Then the radio packed up. Still, it all added a bit of excitement!" His eyes dance as he looks at me. "Now, what are we doing tomorrow? Shopping? Fish and chips on the pier? Or a lovely quiet romantic day, just the two of us . . . ?"

THAT night I didn't sleep much. I just lay there listening to my husband's quiet breathing, thanking all my lucky stars in that clear night sky that he came back safely to me. Oh, I know my life isn't like Sienna's and I don't have six hungry mouths to feed on very little. But being without Dave is unthinkable.

My book was fiction, but people did live in harsh times. Things are changing for everyone; not just for me, but I know one thing — I'll never regret a single moment we share, not ever again.

Now, after a wonderful week here, I sit looking out at the moonlit sea on this, the very last night of our holiday. It's true that the sea can be a very scary place but she brought *The Rosie* and Dave safely home and made me realise how lucky I am, and for that, I'll be grateful for ever.

We've got so much to look forward to, especially here in our little bit of paradise beside the Dorset Seat. The next chapter of our life is just about to begin, and no doubt it will come complete with a whole new set of photos to pin on the wall . . . ■

The Band Of Gold

RAPT in their dreams, they stand, our loving pair,
  Before the jeweller's window . . . What a show
Of lovely rings and necklaces is there,
On tiny cushions, row on sparkling row!
But our young sweethearts never will aspire
To jewels so precious . . . no, their one desire
Is for a ring, a small, plain band of gold,
To bind them together, and bring joy untold.

A little ring, a golden ring
  For Jean to wear with pride.
  No matter what the years
    may bring,
  They'll face it, side by side.
  For two brave hearts
    that beat as one
  Will always stand
    the test,
  And Jean and Hamish
    know for sure
  Their love is
    heaven blessed.
  A love that will
    last a lifetime,
    staunch and
    true,
  And be for ever
    shining, ever
    new.

  And, when the
    ring is bought,
    be sure of
    this . . .
  Hamish will turn
    to Jean, all
    bashful bliss,
  To seal the happy
    moment with a kiss.
— *Kathleen O'Farrell.*

by Cecilia Rose.

Illustration by Kiri Hardy.

46 Church Road,
Dumfries,
Scotland.

DEAR GREAT-GRAN,
Try not to be too shocked when you read this.

I know I've never written a letter to you before, and I can only remember meeting you once, when I was about about eight, but we had a new PSD (Personal and Social Development) teacher today, called Mrs Shields, and that's why I'm writing you this letter!

Anyway, I'm not very good at explaining stuff, so I'll just copy out what she gave us to do for homework.

84

Getting To Know You

Choose an older family member. Find out something about them and how they see the world. You could get them to tell you a story about their past experiences, or share a hobby. Explain why you are asking them and don't forget to thank them for their time.

Well, Mrs Shields was really cool and interesting. She talked about how we only live in a tiny part of our lives — the safe part — and that we don't explore much of the unknown which is just around the corner.

She said that we could discover all kinds of things if we just reached out somehow; if we did something different, or spoke to someone new, and stopped thinking that life is boring (which it is most of the time, by the way). Then I suddenly remembered that you were living in Wales, so I asked Mum for your address when she came home. (Mum says hi, and that she's sorry she forgot your birthday but she's been very busy with the new job.)

Anyway, I actually sat straight down and wrote this. I know it's not very good but, honestly, I've hardly ever written a letter before. I suppose it's because I can phone my pals, or text them on my mobile, or e-mail them — if I can get Paul away from the computer!

I'm sorry I've never written back when you sent cards for my birthday — but thanks for sending them, anyway. I know my mum writes our news on your card at Christmas.

It would be good if you wrote back and told me something about yourself. My mum says there are old photos of you up in the loft, and that she'll look them out when she's got the time, which will be never! I can't really remember what you look like, so the photos will help.

I've sent you a photo of me with my best friend Judi in front of Notre Dame Cathedral on our school trip to France. I'm the small one with the long hair. We both think we look older than thirteen, which is why I sent it to you.

Anyway, this is the most I have written for homework for ages. Mum tells me all the time that I am lazy. I know I am. I just can't be bothered with school.

I hope you are keeping well.

Yours sincerely,
Your great-grandaughter,

Debs.

St Mary's Nursing Home,
Cadoc's Bay,
Pembrokeshire.

My dear Debs,
What a surprise it was to receive your letter by yesterday morning's post! I must admit to having spent the last day pondering the contents and how best to compose my reply.
First of all, I should tell you how delighted I am to hear from my great-granddaughter! I remember our only meeting very clearly. I thought you seemed a very happy child, bursting with energy and full of interest in the world. You told me in no uncertain terms that you wanted to be a vet when you grew up!
I wonder if you remember going out into some large gardens on a very hot summer day and making "the longest daisy chain in the world" while your mother and I chatted. Needless to say, I enjoyed that afternoon immensely.
I believe you are very fortunate to have your new teacher, Mrs Shields. It is a great gift to be able to inspire one's pupils. There is a great deal of wisdom in what she has to say about living in the "safe part of our lives". I have been reflecting on that phrase a great deal since I read your letter, and it has given me much food for thought.
I have been looking back on certain decisions in my life and wondering whether they were decisions to be "safe", rather than anything else. Some were, indeed, "safe" decisions, and one was certainly, "a leap into the unknown".
I have realised today that one of my "safe" decisions was cutting off all contact with your father. I was very fond of Frank, you see, but I'm sure you'll forgive me when I say that he was always a headstrong young lad, full of his own ideas, wanting to change the world.
I watched him court and marry your mother while he was still at university studying medicine, and when he dropped out of the course shortly before you were born, I simply could not forgive him. I felt he was not taking his responsibilities seriously enough.
To me, at that time, my grandson was revealing himself as selfish and unreliable after everything he had been given, and of course, his parents were so hurt and disappointed. They just could not understand him, and neither could I, and so I made my mind up. I suppose I was protecting myself from any unpleasant consequences of his decision.
I see things rather differently now, but it is difficult to alter the status quo.
Your mother, bless her, has been remarkable at keeping in touch with me. The day she brought you for that visit was only the third time I had met her. She broke the journey on the way back from a training course in London.
Well, I have not even begun to answer your letter properly and I must stop

writing. I tire very easily these days. There is so much I want to say to you about your own letter, but it shall have to wait till next time.

I do hope you can decipher my handwriting. I used to be very proud of it, but it has deteriorated recently. The arthritis is in both hands now.

With love,

Great-gran.

P.S. Do you see much of your father? I know he lives some distance away, but perhaps you could pass on my good wishes. I have been remembering how fond I was of him and what stimulating company he was.

Dear Great-gran,

First, thanks a million for writing back so quickly. Your letter has had a mega-effect on my life! I can't believe it! I had no idea my dad was going to be a doctor! Nobody told me. Although now it makes sense, him and Mum always moaning at me to stick in at school.

Honestly, Great-gran, I thought about phoning you 'cos there's so much to tell you! My head's bursting with everything that's happened — but then I thought it would be better if I make myself write the letter and sort out my ideas.

First of all, yes, I do remember making the longest daisy chain in the world and how hot it was, and the visit to London. But I had completely forgotten that I wanted to be a vet! I kind of blanked it out when I went to secondary school and found out that I was rubbish at studying and homework. So I just forgot all about that ambition until you reminded me.

Now that I think of it, I suppose I still would like to work with animals. Maybe I could be a vet's assistant . . . Do they have to study much?

Anyway, the second thing that happened was that I showed your letter to my mum. She read it and didn't say anything for ages, so I said to her, "I didn't know Dad was going to be a doctor. That would have been cool."

And she started crying!

Crying! My mum! She never cries. Not even when Paul got knocked down and he was lying in the road, or at the hospital, or anything. But she read your letter, and started to cry.

I felt really strange then. I can't describe it. It was like seeing my mum as not my mum any more, but just this woman who has to work all hours and who got divorced, and won't ever go out and meet anyone else.

She hardly ever goes to parties, or nights out, or anything. I can hardly remember Dad living at home, anyway, so I've never known things any different.

I just always accepted that Mum works all the time, and we visit Dad once a month — if he's there. We can't stay long 'cos his flat is tiny. It's just always been like that.

Anyway, I made Mum a cup of tea, and she talked to me like I was grown up. She didn't say much, just that she never really stopped loving Dad. Even when they got divorced, she somehow always hoped they'd get back together again, and she decided never to say anything bad about Dad to us, and she never has.

I suddenly saw that my mum is trying her best. I mean *really* trying her best. She's trying a lot harder than I am at the moment. She works so hard at her job — and she does try hard to be a good mum. She *is* a good mum!

Anyway, talking with her made me realise that I could try a bit harder, not moan about school so much and not complain whenever she asks me to do something.

I told her I'd start getting the dinner when she's late back, and I really meant it for once! So, I made the tea on Wednesday, and on Thursday I actually cleaned the bathroom, which is my least favourite housework job of all time.

Funny thing is, when she saw it, she didn't say anything. She just hugged me, and it gave me a really good feeling inside. So I don't mind doing things as much now.

Paul said to me yesterday that I'd had a personality change and that it won't last, but I feel different inside, Great-gran, and it all came from your letter.

The third thing that happened was that we got PSD again and Mrs Shields asked if we wanted to report back. I didn't really feel I wanted to say anything, because it was too personal, but I didn't have to, after all.

Loads of other people had spoken to their grandparents and some of them even had stories to do with the war. For instance, Martin Burns' grandfather had been given a medal for bravery and Martin didn't know a thing about it! It was amazing what people had found out. Gemma Barns had a great-aunt who fell in love with a traveller when she was only seventeen and her father stopped her from seeing him!

Anyway, your letter was fantastic. Have you got any stories of the war? I could maybe tell the class about them if you have.

Thanks for writing back, Great-gran.

Lots of love,
Debs.

P.S. If it's too tiring to write, I could phone you if you want.
P.P.S. I visit Dad next week. I'll tell him you were asking about him.

My dear Debs,

I can't tell you how delighted I was to hear that my letter had had such a positive effect on your situation. Isn't it strange that our actions can have such far-reaching consequences? I am very glad that you have a deeper understanding of your mother's situation, and can help her accordingly.

Leadhills

LEADHILLS and neighbouring Wanlockhead, the two highest villages in Scotland, have a secret beneath them. The Leadhills ore field has drawn people to this inhospitable country since the dawn of history. The Romans mined lead here. By the 16th century, silver was also being produced, and gold was being panned from the river by German experts. Leadhills gold went into the coinage of James V and Mary, Queen of Scots, and was incorporated in regalia both within and outside Scotland.

Local heroes include William Symington, steam navigation pioneer, and Allan Ramsay, poet and bookseller, who founded the first circulating library in Edinburgh.

Then there was mine surveyor John Taylor. On his hundredth birthday his family led him up a big hill so that God might notice him and take him home!

But John had the last laugh. He lived on for over thirty years.

J. CAMPBELL KERR.

A phone call is a lovely idea but, unfortunately, I do not hear very well now; one of the penalties of old age, I'm afraid. So letters are best, even if they do tire me a little.

For the sake of next week's important PSD lesson, I shall tell you, as briefly as I can, a wartime experience of my own that I have never forgotten, and then, if I still have the energy, perhaps I can say some of the other things I intended to.

During the war, I used to travel by train, every Saturday, to my piano teacher, who lived in Cardiff. We had been heavily bombed the night before and none of us had slept much down in the air-raid shelter. Nevertheless, I was determined the next morning not to miss my piano lesson. So I caught my train.

I noticed there was a lot more bustle and activity than usual as I came out of the station; people milling around, police, ARP wardens, and so on, but it was only when I turned into the street where my piano teacher lived that I realised what had happened.

Most of the street had simply disappeared. The houses on both sides were nothing but rubble. I cannot describe to you what I felt. I can only say that it was in that moment that I understood, truly understood, what war meant.

Do you know, Debs, I knew of many other people who lost their lives during those years, and many other tragic circumstances, but when I think of the war, it is always that moment that comes back to me. The whole street, with all that was familiar in it, swept away.

Not perhaps the most cheerful of stories, Debs, but I wanted to pass it on to you. It is such a part of me because, you see, I met your great-grandfather at a dance the following Saturday night. He was on a fortnight's leave and the night we had to say goodbye, he asked me to marry him.

And that was the "leap into the unknown" that I mentioned in my last letter. Without the experience of standing in that devastated street, I would never have had the courage to say yes. I had seen for myself how frail and unpredictable our lives are, and yet here was Robert, asking me to make such a commitment when the world was in turmoil. It gave me back my hope. I had to say yes.

And you know we were happily married, Robert and I. Very happily married! I'm sending you our wedding photograph. You can see how handsome he was.

My dear, I shall have to stop now. My hand is really quite painful and I am rather tired, but I want you to have this letter before your next lesson.

With much love,
Great-gran.

Dear Great-gran,
Your story about the war was really amazing. I told it in the PSD class and

Mrs Shields wants to include it on a video we are going to make called "Explorations".

And guess what! I'm writing this at my dad's. I hope you don't mind but I told him you were asking for him and he wanted to see your letters. Both of them. It was weird, 'cos it was like my mum all over again, except Dad didn't cry. He just sat there for ages looking at the photo you sent and then he asked me if he could add a P.S. at the end of the letter, so I said fine — but he'll have to wait till I'm finished.

Anyway, it's funny, but I've started to enjoy school a lot more since I've taken a leaf out of Mum's book and I'm trying a bit harder. Basically, I'm paying more attention and I've stopped thinking of everything as boring before it starts. Plus, Mum has really cheered up since I've been doing more in the house and, you know, I really don't mind. In fact, I'm enjoying it!

Dad is in the kitchen, having to cope without Kathleen helping him. Apparently she was offered a really good job back in York! She was OK, but I've never really got to know Dad's girlfriends very well. Not that he's had that many. He says he's too busy with his music. Actually, I think Kathleen was more like a friend than anything else. He met her when he was touring the clubs in the north of England and she was singing with him for a while, but he said this was too good an opportunity for her to miss.

He's trying to get another band together. I hope he does soon. It makes all the difference when we come to stay. If Dad's working, we get Chinese take-aways; if he's not, we get beans on toast. Still, I have to admit, he is brilliant on the guitar.

Mum read your letter as well. She said she thought your story was beautiful — that's what she said — *beautiful*. And she said she'd try and bring Paul and me down to see you when she has her next holidays. That'll be June. June's not far away, Great-gran. I'd love to meet you again. It'll be great!

Oops! Here's Dad, trying to read over my shoulder. I'll say 'bye for now.
                              Love,
                              Debs.

P.S. Dear Gran,
Hi!
I have the use of a van next weekend. I could bring Debs down on Saturday if she wants to come. I'll phone to confirm on Friday unless I hear to the contrary.
                              Love,
                              Mike.

P.P.S. Of course I want to come! I'll be there, Great-gran. Definitely! Dad can be so brilliant sometimes.

P.P.P.S. Dad has just gone into the kitchen again, but I'm adding this extra bit because I can't believe what's just happened! Please excuse the writing, but my hand has gone all shaky with excitement.

Dad laughed when I hugged him and wrote that he was brilliant, but then he said to me, "How did you do it, Debs? I never thought she'd come round, not after all these years."

Well, do you know, Great-gran, I never thought. I just went into my schoolbag and gave him my copies of the letters I'd written to you. Both of them! It wasn't until he was halfway through them that I realised what I'd done. There was all that stuff I'd written about my mum and how she felt and everything. My heart started beating really fast because I felt terrible for Mum, as if I'd given her away somehow, but it was too late to do anything about it, so I just sat there and kept quiet.

Dad didn't say anything for ages and then he said, "Do you think your mum would want to come with us on Saturday, and bring Paul as well?" That's what he said! And he didn't look at me, he just waited, as if my answer was really important to him. So I took a deep breath and said, "I could ask her, if you like."

And he said, "You do that, Debs. You ask her for me." Then he kind of ruffled my hair and hugged me really hard, and he laughed and said I was the one who was brilliant, not him!

Now all I have to do is ask Mum, and I think she'll say yes. In fact, knowing Mum, she's bound to say yes!

I can't believe it, Great-gran! The four of us, coming to see you — together!

See you soon,
Lots and lots of love,
Debs.

P.P.P.P.S. You know, Mrs Shields is a really, really brilliant teacher. We start making the "Explorations" video tomorrow. I never ever thought I'd say this, but I'm actually looking forward to going to school!

Getting To Know You

The Cottage Guest-house,
Netherhill,
Lake Windermere.

Dear Great-gran,

I'm sitting up in bed writing this at two o'clock in the morning and, as you can see, I'm not even at home! I know you said you would write next because it was your turn, but it's been such an incredible day, I wanted to share the ending of it with you.

It was fantastic meeting you again, especially after everything that's happened, but I think you know that. What I couldn't tell you when I first saw you was that Mum and Dad hardly spoke a word to each other on the journey down in the van.

Dad did try to chat, but Mum just didn't seem to be able to talk, so we listened to the radio instead. Paul didn't notice. He was too interested in getting to the next level on his Gameboy.

By the time we reached Wales, I was getting really worried. They did talk about directions and which route to take, but it was all a bit strained. That's the real reason why I looked pale when we arrived. I know I said I'd been feeling carsick but it was really just worry about whether I'd done the right thing, especially for Mum.

You see, I decided not to tell her that I'd shown Dad my letters. I thought if she knew he'd read them, she might not want to come down with us after all. But then, when she was so quiet with Dad, I began to realise that Dad knew something about Mum she might never have told him, or wanted him to know, and he was — well, there was something different about him, and if I noticed, then Mum would notice, too.

I thought that maybe it was all going wrong. But then we met you, and everything changed.

I could see Dad was so pleased to see you, and Mum was pleased to see him happy. Of course, your suggestion that we all go along for lunch to the King's Arms, instead of eating in the dining-room, really helped.

Mum began to relax when you got her talking about her painting, and Dad was very nice to her about it, and encouraged her to get her easel down from the loft — so that helped as well. Plus Paul loved throwing sticks for Honey, that daft Labrador, so that kept him occupied for ages.

But the real clever thing was later on, when you asked Dad to play his guitar for the residents. I would never have thought of it myself, but in no time at all Mum was singing along to help get everyone going, and suggesting stuff for him to play that everyone would know. And, of course, I'd forgotten that Mum had such a lovely voice. It was just brilliant to hear her singing again.

I had another of those strange moments, Great-gran, when I was watching

93

them, Dad on his guitar and Mum calling out the words ahead of the tune. It was as if they weren't my parents any more, just two people, smiling and laughing and looking as if they belonged together.

As you know, we left a lot later than we intended. We'd driven for about an hour, when Dad said to Mum, "Do you have to be home tonight? Are you working tomorrow?"

And Mum said she had Sunday off. So then Dad said why didn't we all stay overnight at this little bed and breakfast place he knew in the Lake District. Of course, Paul was desperate to stop anywhere, and I said I thought it was a great idea. There was a long pause, and then Mum said, "It is getting very late. I suppose it does make sense to stop."

So, instead of heading for Scotland as quickly as possible, we turned off the motorway into the countryside and we ended up at this beautiful little guest-house on the banks of Lake Windermere.

We had supper sitting in the garden watching the sun set over the water and wonderful mountains in the distance.

I dragged Paul off for a walk when we'd finished eating (honestly, Paul can be so thick sometimes!) and when we came back, guess what? Dad was composing a song on the guitar and Mum was helping him make up the words!

That's why I can't sleep, Great-gran. They're still sitting chatting together right now, and I'm too happy to sleep. Can you imagine that? Too happy to sleep?

I'm stuck sharing a room with Paul, but that doesn't matter. He zonked out about eleven o'clock.

I think it is dawning on him that Mum and Dad are getting on well, but I've found out that nine-year-old boys seem to take this kind of thing in their stride.

Anyway, I'm here, in this lovely old-fashioned little room and I wanted to tell you all about it, because if it wasn't for you, and visiting you, and how you seemed to know exactly what to do with both of them today, then none of this would have happened.

So thank you, thank you, thank you, Great-gran!

With lots and lots of love,

Your very happy great-granddaughter,

Debs.

P.S. One of the things Dad and Mum talked about on the way up was how to visit you more often, so I don't think it'll be too long before we see each other again.

I'll look forward to your next letter.

Love again,

D.

WHEN I was eleven, I hoped never to meet Niall O'Donnell again.

Now, at twenty-eight, I barely recognised the scrawny, sharp-elbowed annoyance I remembered. With his tousled fair hair and beautiful, sparkling eyes, was it too much to ask that he would no longer see the scowling, clumsy girl I had been?

"Kate!" He beamed, enveloping me in a warm hug before holding me at arm's length for a better look. "You've hardly changed at all."

* * * *

We were thrown together when our families shared a holiday home on the Antrim coast in Northern Ireland. Our mothers had been school friends, and stayed in touch after mine left for married life in Scotland.

The weather was unusually kind, granting us day after day on vast, unspoilt

Do Wishes Come True?

by
Rebecca
Holmes.

Illustration by André Leonard.

beaches. There were sandcastles to be built, an ocean to be conquered, and picnics to be devoured with the appetite that sea air bestows. It would have been the perfect holiday, if it hadn't been for the constant thorn in my side.

Clever-clogs Niall always had to know better than me, whether we were collecting shells — and he could name them all — or throwing ourselves against the waves.

Even at the house there was no escape. Whenever I would sneak away to read, or watch the horses in the adjacent field and imagine they were mine, he would be there. I wished he'd just leave me alone. He was a nuisance, a know-it-all, and I didn't like him.

On the morning it was announced we were to visit the Giant's Causeway, I handed over my swimming costume to be packed along with the other provisions, as usual. Niall, the big-head, could barely contain his mirth.

"You won't be needing that, silly. There's no beach there." He pulled a face at me when the grown-ups weren't looking.

"No beach? Then what's the point in going?"

"Because it's a *very* famous place. *World* famous. Haven't you heard of it?"

I had, but it meant nothing to me. Why waste a baking hot day wandering round a pile of old rocks, I thought, when the blue sea beckoned?

It's a wonder I didn't get a clipped ear to add to my troubles, the way I sulked. No towering cliffs and grand scenery were going to impress me, especially with my new-found fear of heights.

Niall kept showing off, of course.

"Oh, look," he said. "There's the Giant's Organ. And aren't those cliffs the Giant's Cuffs?"

If he'd pointed out the Giant's Toenails, I wouldn't have been surprised.

"Do either of you know who the Giant was?" My "uncle" George intervened.

HE told us about Finn MacCool tearing pieces from the cliffs to build a causeway across the water to reach his enemy, Finn Gall. And of how he needed to rest but, knowing the Scottish giant would come looking for him, disguised himself as a baby. The trick worked. Not prepared to face a giant the size of this "baby's" father, Finn Gall fled home, destroying the causeway as he went.

"And what you see now is what was left."

I frowned.

"How did all of this really get made?"

"Now you're asking, Kate. The rocks were formed by volcanoes, I know that much."

"But what about these?" I pointed to the ground. The surface of the rock was made up of six-sided shapes, so regular that they could have been put together deliberately.

"The cracks, you mean? That's where it gets more complicated. Any ideas, Niall?"

Niall shrugged his shoulders.

"I only know what you've told us, Da."

He didn't know! I could have skipped with delight, but settled instead for deciding that once I was home I would solve the mystery. Despite myself, I realised I wanted to find out more.

What with all the chat and story-telling, we soon reached our destination and spread the rug for yet another picnic. It felt strange to be eating sausage rolls and chocolate cake in such spellbinding surroundings. Some of the basalt columns still stood vertically; others were tumbled about, giving the scene a haphazard appearance.

"Aren't you going to sit in the Giant's Chair and make a wish?" Uncle George asked. "Now surely you've heard about that?"

Instinctively, and to our mutual surprise, Niall and I glanced at each other as if both seeking guidance on how to react. We were at that age when adults still fondly expected us to believe in such things, and sometimes we'd indulge them.

"I'll give it a try," I ventured.

I stood up and gingerly made my way, up and down in uneven steps, over the rocks to the "chair". Sitting on the sun-warmed stone, I gazed to the horizon and wished for my heart's desire, one probably shared with many girls my age.

The sound of the waves and the sharp salt smell made me light-headed for a moment, and it was almost possible to believe that my wish might come true . . .

"I'll have a go, if you're done."

I hadn't noticed Niall approach. He took his turn, trying to look nonchalant, but I saw how he clenched his fists and screwed up his eyes when he thought I wasn't looking.

Afterwards, we didn't really talk, and we certainly didn't tell each other what we had wished for.

THE holiday ended soon after, and no more were arranged, so there was no need for me to break up any causeways on the ferry home.

I fulfilled my promise to myself, though, discovering how rivers of molten lava had rushed into the sea and been quickly cooled by the water — hissing and cracking, and crystallising into hexagonal columns which still remain standing, millions of years later. The mystery was solved, in a way I found more satisfying than any tale of giants.

As for my wish in the Giant's Chair, I soon dismissed that as childish nonsense.

Our mothers still wrote, albeit spasmodically, so I heard that the family had moved to Antrim to run a hotel in one of the small seaside towns there. I concentrated on my own life and notching up various achievements. As time went by, Niall faded to become just another memory, until I could think of him without rancour.

So much so, in fact, that when "Aunt" Mary relayed the news of his being jilted — virtually at the altar — I almost shared her indignation.

If I had my way, Bernadette, the letter to my mother read, *I'd tell that girl a few home truths. But Niall won't hear a word against her. My only consolation is that her parents are paying the bills.*

My own mother, not to be outdone, made a point of mentioning my long line of failed romances, as she saw them. None were serious; I just hadn't found anyone special. But my mother didn't see it quite like that.

Well, as you know, she can be such a contrary girl. She frightens them all off, Mum wrote — so I suppose, in a way, Niall and I were just about even.

The "Friend" Remembers Wartime Chanteuses & Entertainers

Dame Gracie Fields 1898 — 1979

WASN'T she a bonnie Lancashire lass? Dame Gracie Fields was born in Rochdale, and during her early years she worked as a part-timer in a local cotton mill. By the age of ten, she was touring with singing and dancing groups, and by sixteen she was starring in the revue "Yes, I Think So" at Hulme, Manchester.

During the Thirties, Gracie was arguably one of the most famous women in Britain, with crowds gathering wherever she appeared. With typical modesty, though, she described herself as "an ordinary woman with an extraordinary voice".

Known as "Our Gracie", she became one of the country's top music hall attractions.

Her long career spanned radio, recordings, television and films such as "Sally In Our Alley" (1931) and "Sing As We Go" (1934). Gracie made fifteen films between 1931 and 1946.

After her London debut in Drury Lane, her comical songs, "The Biggest Aspidistra In The World" and "My Sister's Young Man Is One Hundred And Three" were heard on radios everywhere.

World War II broke out when Dame Gracie was at the peak of her career, and she immediately made plans for a concert tour for the British Expeditionary Forces in France.

In her broadcast concert from "somewhere in France" she sang "Ave Maria" and "Wish Me Luck As You Wave Me Goodbye". She also took on a legendary six-week tour from Scapa Flow to Plymouth, giving three performances a day in Army

All of this meant that when I finally returned to Ireland, this time working on a coastline survey, the prospect of boarding at the O'Donnells' guesthouse held no fear. In fact, after the first few awkward moments, I really enjoyed it. With all of our childhood differences forgotten, we could start again on a

Gracie Fields

and Air Force camps and also in factories.

Gracie emigrated to America with her husband Monty Banks in 1940, but she made return visits to Britain throughout her life and gave many concerts.

Dame Gracie was awarded the CBE in 1938 and a DBE in 1978. She was well known for her generosity, devoting a large part of her income to charity.

fresh footing.

Even so, I was surprised when Niall turned up at the beach one day as I took photographs and collected samples.

"All part of the service," he told me. "I noticed you'd come out without your lunch, so I've brought it for you, along with a flask of good, strong coffee."

He'd brought enough for two, so we sat on the rocks and watched the waves roll back with the turning tide as we ate.

"How did you know where I was?"

"I didn't, but I know the beaches round here. I just narrowed it down to the most likely ones. Happening to see which way you turned at the bottom of the drive also helped!"

I felt briefly uncomfortable at the thought that he might have been watching me, but the feeling soon passed, helped by the fact that the prawn sandwiches he had brought were delicious — infinitely preferable to the chocolate bar in my pocket which would have been my meal otherwise.

After that day, he turned up regularly — occasionally setting out with me in the morning so that we spent the whole day together. There was no worry about abandoning the hotel. Mary, as I felt able to call her now, was always willing to take over when required. She even seemed happy to encourage our frequent excursions.

"George and I ran this place ourselves for years," she told me one evening whilst I was taking a break from entering my findings on to my laptop.

"I enjoy keeping my hand in, now I don't have to do it all the time. And," she added, in a low voice, "I'm glad to see Niall out and about again. He's shut himself away too much, these past few months. It's about time he got on with living again."

Despite working conscientiously, the project took longer than I'd expected. I recorded a wealth of information, and was extremely grateful for the aid of my willing helper who, in his faded corduroys and battered windcheater, seemed to take a childish delight in leaving size ten footprints across the sand. He knew many of the beaches intimately, and was able to show me hidden coves that I would never have discovered otherwise.

"You find these places gradually, over time," he said. "I used to spend the school holidays exploring on my bike, with my swimming trunks wrapped in a towel and a couple of sandwiches for lunch. It's come in useful in the long run. Guests often ask for advice, and I can warn them where it's not safe to swim.

"There are so many strong currents around this coast, it's all too easy to get swept away before you realise what's happening."

I loved every moment of my stay, even though the weather was very different from when I'd been here before. It was cold and wild — everything you'd expect from the ravages of autumn sliding into winter.

In many ways, Niall and I were different, too, both shaped by the passing years like cliffs eroded by the ocean. But spray and mist can hide the full picture until the air clears with the arrival of spring. Sadly, we didn't have that long.

O N my last day, we couldn't resist going back to the Giant's Causeway. "After all," Niall said, "it's such a famous place, it would be a sin not to visit."

"*World* famous, don't you mean?"

"It is indeed." He grinned. "Have you got your swimming costume?"

My heart lifted at the sight of the ancient columns and honeycomb pavements. This "pile of old rocks" was where so much had started for me — sparking my curiosity and eventually leading me to this job, which I loved. Without them, I could have ended up bored, in an office somewhere, which just wasn't me.

"I still like the story about the giants," Niall mused. "You can understand how people used it as a way to make sense of the place. Sometimes I think it's a shame Finn Gall destroyed the causeway. Who knows? They might have mellowed with age and got together over a glass of whisky."

"Or murdered each other," I said wryly.

The sun hung low in the sky as we gazed across the water towards my homeland. For some reason, it didn't stir the usual feelings in me. Possibly I was distracted by the heavy black clouds that were heading our way, eerily putting half the scene in light, the other half in shadow.

I sighed.

"It seems strange to think I'm going back tomorrow. It's like another life."

"So stay," Niall said.

I must have looked as astounded as I felt, because he hesitated and cleared his throat.

"Or come and visit again. The sea air does you good, and it's not too far to travel."

Within a split second, my mood swung from being a little melancholy but peaceful to one of turmoil. My reaction, as ever, was to go on the defensive.

"It might not be far, as the crow flies, but would you fancy making that crossing in bad weather? And as for sea air, I get plenty of that in my job, anyway!"

I caught a glimpse of Niall's eyes then, and just for an instant, I saw how much hurt lay under the surface. If I could have taken back my words, I would. Yet what would I have said? I felt out of my depth, unused to situations that couldn't be solved by examining them under a microscope.

It was too late, anyway. Niall's shutters were down. When he spoke, his voice sounded devoid of emotion.

"We'd better be moving," he said, nodding towards the clouds. "The Land-Rover's a good ten minutes away."

As we rushed back ahead of the blackening sky, I could just make out the position of the Giant's Chair in the distance, surrounded by its companion rocks. Neither of us commented, as if we had both long abandoned such fanciful notions.

That night, unable to sleep, I stood at the window and watched the moon, during breaks in the clouds, cast its pale light over the silent fields. If I thought such stillness would calm me, I was mistaken.

On several occasions over the past few weeks, I had caught myself thinking of Niall as more than a friend. Sometimes a look or gesture would make me wonder if he felt the same, too. But a voice at the back of my mind would persuade me otherwise.

Remember what he said about getting swept away by the currents, I thought. And it would only make life more complicated. Best leave things as they are, surely?

I had always thought of this as my voice of reason, and never questioned its wisdom . . .

I ended up making a deal with myself. In the morning, if Niall asked me to return, I would. If he didn't, I would head for home.

There was no sign of him at breakfast, where guests held murmured conversations and cutlery clinked against china. He wasn't there, either, when I handed in my keys and paid my bill.

"So you're off?" Mary passed back my credit card.

I nodded, busy sorting out the contents of my purse.

"I see." There was the tiniest pause. "Well, I suppose it was no more than I expected. Give my regards to your mother, won't you? Perhaps she'd like to come over, some time." She sighed and shook her head.

"Bernadette was right — you'll never learn."

It seemed a strange way to say goodbye. As I walked to the door, I couldn't help looking back. Niall's mother was still behind the desk, watching me.

"I'm sorry about Niall's wedding and . . . everything," I said. "But we all have to follow our own path in life."

"I know that, Kate," she replied. "But when you've lived as long as I have, you'll know it isn't always a case of ploughing straight on. If we'd done that, we'd never have taken the plunge and come to Antrim."

THE sky was swollen as I travelled faster than was prudent along the narrow lanes between water-logged fields. Following Mary's directions, I soon came across Niall's Land-Rover parked on the grass verge by the track to the house where we had stayed that summer, so many years ago.

I found him stroking a chestnut mare with a white blaze on her intelligent face. Two other ponies grazed nearby.

The last few yards towards him felt like the longest walk of my life.

"You'll miss your ferry," he said as I drew level.

A seagull screeched mournfully somewhere in the distance.

"There'll be others." The ponies had noticed me and were making their way over. Their coats had already started thickening for the winter.

"I didn't know you liked horses."

He exaggerated his accent.

"Sure, how can I be a true Irishman and not like them?"

Caernarvon Castle, Wales

HERE we can enjoy one of the most famous views of Wales. Situated down by the harbour, Caernarvon is one of Britain's biggest castles, commanding a wonderful view from the top of the Eagle Tower over to Anglesey and down the peninsula.

J. CAMPBELL KERR.

A sudden gust rippled the grass and blew my hair across my face. I waited until it died down, glad of the extra time to gather my courage. If I didn't say something now, I might as well leave.

"Why didn't you stay to see me off?"

"After yesterday? Give me credit for having *some* pride." He looked away, hunching his shoulders and shoving his hands in his pockets.

"You never listened when I knew you before, Kate. You always had to do things your way. Yet, when I saw you again, I knew I wanted us to be together — even though recent events hadn't exactly helped my confidence.

"I hoped you'd changed, but you kept charging off on your own tack, never content with simply seeing what was before you. And you're still as prickly as the sea urchins we kept finding in all those rock pools. Yesterday just confirmed it."

"But I *have* changed," I protested. "Oh, I know I've made a mess of it all, but I'm here now."

"You mean you've not just come to say goodbye?"

"Not unless you want me to — which I really hope isn't the case."

I STEPPED forward and gently cupped my hand against his face. That was enough. Before I knew it, his arms were round me. Explanations were pushed aside as our embrace told us more than a thousand words could say. We only drew apart when the mare, feeling ignored, tossed her head and snorted loudly at us.

"Someone's jealous." Niall produced some mints from his pocket and fed one to her as she nuzzled his sleeve.

"Has she a name?"

"Amber," he said. "Isn't she lovely?"

"She's gorgeous," I breathed.

"Her owner's thinking of selling her, if you're interested. Of course, that would only apply if you were coming back." He winked.

I couldn't help it. I laughed out loud. I laughed until the tears rolled down my cheeks.

Niall was dumbfounded.

"What's so funny?"

"Do you remember our first visit to the Giant's Causeway?" I asked.

He nodded.

"What of it?"

"What did you wish for, on the Giant's Chair?"

"I wished I could live here and never leave." He smiled. "And you?"

It had started raining again, but we hardly noticed. This time it was Niall's turn to roar with laughter as I told him how I'd wished for a pony.

Do wishes come true? I think so — even if they're not always what we imagine! ∎

A Labour Of Love

I'M Jessie McPhee, such a busy
  old bee,
For when there's a wedding,
  they send for me,
And I was so
  pleased when I
  heard them say,
"Jean and Hamish
  have named
  the day."

For I have a
  touch with
  pies and
  such,
My pastry
  melts in the
  mouth like
  snow,
And I can bake a
  magnificent
  cake,
Perfect for weddings, I'll have
  you know.
"Nobody cooks like Jessie McPhee,"
I've heard folks say — and I must agree.

For each and all of us have our share
Of gifts, and my special one, it seems,
Is being competent to prepare
Delicious dishes, the stuff of dreams.

And I'm honoured, and truly glad this day,
To be hard at work on the wedding fare,
For Jeanie's parents, good neighbours they,
Have little of worldly wealth to spare.
For them, I will serve up the very best
Of wedding breakfasts, so every guest
Will say, "This wedding beats all the rest!"
— **Kathleen O'Farrell.**

The First Day Of

"M UM, is my PE kit ready?" Sam, football mad and ten years old, yelled.

"Mum, have you made my packed lunch?" Jack, Ellie's ever-hungry seven-year-old, called.

"Ellie, have you seen my briefcase? I can't remember where I put it last night."

That came from Roger, her thirty-something husband — who should know better.

Amidst all the noise and commotion, Ellie bit her lip and deliberately refilled the kettle. It was either that or scream loud and long if someone else so much as uttered her name. She hated the first day of school.

No matter how much she tried to prepare herself, it was always organised chaos as everyone struggled to get back into the normal routine, reluctantly leaving the freedom of summer holidays far behind.

Ellie stole a glance at breakfast television, where the presenter was waxing lyrical about his upcoming late break to the Caribbean. How wonderful would that be? Sun, sea, time to chill out and relax, with no demanding kids, no irritable husband — a far cry from the week spent in her parents' caravan in August, when it had rained non-stop for three days.

"Mummy, can I have some cereal?"

Ellie turned from the sight of cocktails and palm trees to smile at Sophie, her three-year-old daughter, and sole female ally in this house of demanding males. Even the cat was a huffy tom which only ate the most expensive cat food on the market.

"Sure you can, sweetheart. Is that enough?"

Sophie nodded her consent at the half-filled bowl and climbed on to a stool, chattering nineteen to the dozen as Ellie poured the milk.

"Thanks, Mummy." Sophie's ear-splitting grin through a mouthful of cereal was enough to brighten the darkest of days. Ellie couldn't help giving an answering smile, a smile that wavered when it suddenly hit her that the boys weren't the only ones heading off to school. Sophie, her little sweetheart, was starting nursery today.

Ellie was momentarily distracted from her gloom by the chaos in the hall, which was building to a crescendo as the boys clattered down the

106

School

Illustration by
Steve Caldwell.

by Karen
Maxwell.

107

stairs with their various bags while Roger performed his usual frenzied hunt for his car keys and mobile phone. Some things never changed, no matter what day it was.

"Ellie, where's . . .?"

"On the hall table where you left them."

"Oh, right, thanks. OK, boys, are you ready to go? We don't want to be late."

There was the usual flurry of kisses, hugs and good luck wishes as they bundled out *en masse* into the car like a herd of elephants.

"Oh, Ellie, before I forget, could you pick my suit up from the dry-cleaner's? I've an important meeting tomorrow."

"OK."

She waved to the kids and wearily kissed Roger goodbye. She loved her husband dearly, but sometimes he was a real pain in the neck! What she really wanted to say was "Get it yourself." But what would be the point? Roger wouldn't even know where the dry-cleaner's was — or the supermarket, or the butcher's, or anywhere else for that matter. The boys were as bad — as long as they were fed and watered that was all they cared about.

SUPPRESSING a heavy sigh, Ellie turned to survey her abandoned house. It would take her the best part of the morning to get the place straight. Boy, but she hated Mondays!

Leaving Sophie to finish her cereal, she charged through the house like a whirlwind, making beds, lifting damp towels, putting dirty washing in the laundry basket — instead of leaving it on the floor where male members of the species seemed convinced it belonged.

A quick glance at her watch showed there was barely fifteen minutes before she needed to leave for Sophie's all-important first day, and the poor child was still in her pyjamas. Fighting down the lump in her throat, she dressed her daughter in jeans and the signature red sweatshirt with the "Little Acorns" logo.

"There you go, sweetie. Don't you look smart?"

As well as the lump, her eyes had decided to water in sympathy at the sight of Sophie, so grown up. Where had the time gone? It seemed like only yesterday when she'd brought that little pink bundle home.

"Will Anna be there, Mummy?" For the first time Sophie sounded slightly anxious as they drove the couple of miles to the church hall which housed the local playgroup.

Ellie glanced protectively at her little daughter in the rear-view mirror.

"Of course, she will — and Jack, and Susie, and lots of others from mothers and toddlers."

She was quick to reassure, hiding her own anxiety at the thought of leaving Sophie on her own. Maybe she'd fret, or start to cry? What if she wouldn't let

108

her leave? What if she couldn't bring *herself* to go?

"Oh, goody, I can't wait! Oh, look, Mummy, there's Anna's car in front! Can I go in with her?"

So much for her baby being anxious and worried about leaving her mummy. Miss Independent couldn't wait to get out of her booster seat and see her friend, skipping into the hall with only a brief kiss and fleeting wave for her poor abandoned mother.

"See you later, Mummy."

"See you later, Sophie. Be a good girl and enjoy yourself."

She already was — giggling in the Wendy house with Anna and a host of other energetic three-year-olds, all clearly determined to have a whale of a time without any over-protective parents cramping their style.

"Bye, Sophie." Ellie quietly blew her nose and dabbed her eyes. "Blasted cold," she muttered, hurrying back to her car.

The short drive home was uneventful and quiet — very quiet. No nursery rhymes, no Tweenies tape, no chatter.

The house, too, was silent, although it still looked like a bomb had hit it — dirty dishes left in the sink, a pile of washing waiting to go into the machine.

But before she could even think of getting stuck in, she needed a large cup of coffee to kick-start her day. Cleaner and housekeeper was all she was now — at least until noon, when she had to pick Sophie up.

THE kettle clicked off and Ellie determinedly made herself the promised mug of coffee and sat down at the kitchen table. Mmm! The coffee might only be instant, but it tasted like heaven, and easing her feet out of her shoes, she pulled last night's newspaper towards her.

It was ridiculous! She felt like a naughty schoolgirl bunking off class. She helped herself to a chocolate biscuit and deliberately turned her gaze away from the sink. The dishes could wait. Ellie wanted to read the review of the latest blockbuster to hit the big screen, and that article on weekend breaks to the country . . .

A weekend break. Mmm! She couldn't remember the last time she'd had a break from the daily grind of cooking, cleaning, minding the kids . . .

Suddenly Ellie paused, coffee cup halfway to her mouth as the penny slowly dropped.

Hold on a minute — an uninterrupted cup of coffee, a peaceful house, the paper to herself? Who needed a weekend break or an expensive holiday to the Caribbean when she had all the peace and quiet she needed right here?

With an ear-splitting grin she refilled the kettle and sat back down. There was plenty of time for a long, lazy refill, and after she'd read the paper maybe she'd even give her friend Janet a call for a good old girly chat?

The morning stretched ahead delightfully. Perhaps this first day of school lark wasn't so bad after all! ■

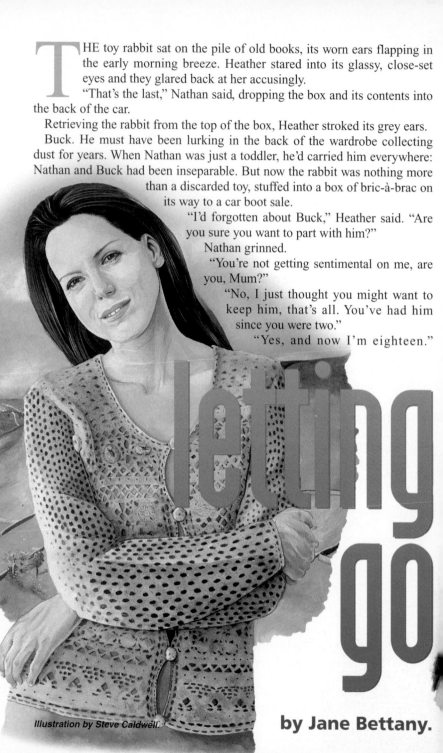

THE toy rabbit sat on the pile of old books, its worn ears flapping in the early morning breeze. Heather stared into its glassy, close-set eyes and they glared back at her accusingly.

"That's the last," Nathan said, dropping the box and its contents into the back of the car.

Retrieving the rabbit from the top of the box, Heather stroked its grey ears.

Buck. He must have been lurking in the back of the wardrobe collecting dust for years. When Nathan was just a toddler, he'd carried him everywhere: Nathan and Buck had been inseparable. But now the rabbit was nothing more than a discarded toy, stuffed into a box of bric-à-brac on its way to a car boot sale.

"I'd forgotten about Buck," Heather said. "Are you sure you want to part with him?"

Nathan grinned.

"You're not getting sentimental on me, are you, Mum?"

"No, I just thought you might want to keep him, that's all. You've had him since you were two."

"Yes, and now I'm eighteen."

letting
go

Illustration by Steve Caldwell.

by Jane Bettany.

Nathan laughed. "My days of playing with toy rabbits are over, Mum.

"I can't afford to be sentimental. When I get to university I'll need all the money I can lay my hands on. If someone's willing to give me a pound for Buck at the car boot sale, then I'll take it."

Heather was pleased that Nathan had finally managed to sort out the chaotic pile of junk that had accumulated in his bedroom. She admired his decision to sell it all off at a car boot sale to raise money for university. But she was surprised at how easily he could part with his favourite toy. Surely Buck must mean something to him if he'd kept him for all these years?

As she continued to stroke Buck's floppy ears, Wilf emerged from the house with a flask in his hand.

"I thought you might appreciate some coffee," he said.

"Thanks, Dad." Nathan smiled.

"I bet you wish you were coming with us, eh?"

"I'm absolutely heartbroken." Wilf grinned. "Missing out on all the fun — it's a real shame there isn't room for me in the car."

"Room is money," Nathan quipped. "If we took you along, we'd have to leave behind at least three boxes."

"And then I suppose we'd be stuck with your old junk for ever," Wilf said.

Laughing, Nathan took the flask from his father and climbed into the passenger seat of the car.

Wilf extracted Buck, who had somehow nestled his way deep into Heather's arms, and dropped him back into the box before closing the boot.

"Are you OK, love?" he asked.

Heather shrugged and gave him a weak smile.

"I'm fine," she replied. "I'm just a bit sad, that's all. It's the end of an era, isn't it? Our little boy all grown up and off to university . . . he doesn't even want Buck any more."

"I should hope not." Wilf grinned. "He'd look a bit odd, wouldn't he, turning up at the halls of residence with an old toy rabbit?"

Wilf could always find a way to make her laugh but, even so, as Heather climbed into the car, waved goodbye to Wilf, and drove off into the village where the car boot sale was to be held, she couldn't completely shake off her sense of melancholy.

She supposed it was natural to have mixed emotions about her only child leaving home — feelings of love, all tangled up with the knowledge of how much she'd miss him.

Heather had always tried to avoid being one of those clingy, over-protective mothers. She and Wilf had done their best to instil a sense of confidence

111

and adventure in their son, and they both viewed his achievements at school and his impending departure as something to be celebrated.

The only thing that really bothered Heather was whether Nathan was adequately prepared for his new life. His childhood in a small village, miles from anywhere, had been idyllic in many ways, allowing him to develop a rich appreciation of the gentler side of life.

But when he set off for Bristol at the end of September, would Nathan be able to cope with living in a big city? Would urban life change him for ever? Make him hard, and ruthless, and grasping?

Heather had spoken to Wilf about her concerns and had even broached the subject with Nathan, but they thought she was worrying over nothing.

"I'll admit that city life might harden him up a bit," Wilf had said. "But that isn't necessarily a bad thing, love. And he'll always be our son, won't he?"

Nathan had laughed.

"They'll probably think I'm a country bumpkin, Mum. But don't worry. I'll survive."

WHEN they arrived at the village sports ground there were already a dozen sellers and a sizeable crowd of buyers. It was a glorious morning, perfect for a car boot sale.

Heather and Nathan unloaded the wobbly pasting table that was to serve as their stall and began to pile it up with items. When one or two impatient buyers started poking around in the back of the car, Nathan asked them firmly, but politely, to wait until they had finished unpacking.

"Dealers," he muttered. "Keep your eye on them, Mum."

How Nathan knew about these things was a mystery to Heather, but she was grateful that he had taken charge. Before long, they had laid out the huge selection of books, toys, games, CDs and ornaments that Nathan had chosen to dispose of.

Heather had surreptitiously pushed Buck down on to the back seat of the car, hoping that Nathan would forget about him. But it wasn't long before he'd retrieved the rabbit and posed him appealingly in the centre of the pasting table.

By ten o'clock the sun was hotter and Heather realised that she was enjoying herself. The smell of warm grass, freshly crushed underfoot, and the happy chattering crowd reminded her of Nathan's school sports days.

Smiling at her memories, Heather looked at Nathan now, still only eighteen, but confidently haggling with customers and chatting with the teenage girls who were lingering flirtatiously at the stall. He would always be a charmer.

At noon he went off to buy food from the burger stand, and when he came back with hot dogs smothered with mustard and fried onions, he and Heather ate them together as if they were a great treat.

The crowds were thinning out now and a few people had already begun to pack up and go home.

112

And still Buck hadn't been sold. Heather smiled secretly to herself. It wasn't surprising really, she thought; with his beady eyes and lopsided ears, he wasn't exactly a handsome rabbit.

She and Nathan had agreed to donate any unsold items to the village jumble sale, but Heather decided that when they got home she would rescue Buck and put him away in the attic.

"We ought to start packing up," Nathan said. "I don't think we're going to sell much more now."

Heather was just about to nod in agreement when a red-haired, freckle-faced boy of about four skipped up to their stall and, smiling shyly, picked up the rabbit and fiddled with its ears. The boy's mother, who had been inspecting some of Nathan's discarded CDs, beamed nostalgically when she saw the rabbit.

"He's like the one you used to have, isn't he, Rod?"

Rod nodded and continued to play with Buck's ears.

The woman and Heather exchanged knowing smiles.

"He cried for days when he lost his old rabbit," the woman whispered. "It took him weeks to get over it."

"Can I buy it, Mummy?" the little boy asked.

"No, Rod. You've already spent your pocket money . . . and besides, you don't *really* want a rabbit, do you? Haven't you grown a bit too old for soft toys?"

Rod continued to cling to Buck, appealing to his mother with sad blue eyes.

"Technically, this rabbit isn't for sale any more. But we are looking for a new home for him, aren't we, Mum?"

Heather stared at Nathan, open-mouthed. But understanding immediately what he was planning, she assumed a look of mock seriousness and nodded.

"That's right," she agreed. "His name's Buck and he needs someone to take care of him, because my son's going away to university in a few weeks."

"He's yours if you'd like him," Nathan said to Rod. "Free of charge, providing you promise to give him lots of cuddles."

Rod's face broke into a broad grin and he hugged the rabbit tightly, as if he were afraid that Nathan might change his mind.

Suddenly, Heather remembered the boy's mother.

"If that's all right with you, of course," she added. "Can you accommodate a homeless rabbit?"

The woman grinned and ruffled Rod's hair.

"I'm sure we'll find room for him. Now, Rod, what do you say?"

Rod looked at Nathan and gave him a sweet, shiny smile.

"Thank you," he said. "I promise I'll look after him."

As the boy disappeared with the rabbit cradled in his arms, Heather felt a hard ball of emotion gather in her throat — not because they had finally said goodbye to Buck, but because she felt moved by her son's kindness.

She knew no matter what happened to him in the big city, he would always make her proud. ■

"WE'RE so lucky!" Jerry exclaimed as he struggled to bend down on one knee.

I smiled. Jerry always made me smile.

"We're so lucky," he repeated, a little flushed in the face, "in both love and life. We've worked so hard. We deserve this."

Well, I wasn't going to argue with any of that, but I did have to ask one thing.

"Are you sure you're all right, kneeling down like that at your age?"

"What do you mean 'at my age?' I'm a young man," he replied, pretending to be offended, and I couldn't help laughing. He'd been my young man for the past sixty-one years now.

We met when we were both nineteen. We married at twenty. Today was our sixtieth anniversary, our diamond wedding.

Looking at him now, scrabbling in his pockets for the ring box that he lost every year without fail, I could still see my nineteen-year-old sweetheart. All those years had only made him more dear to me, in spite of the wrinkles he'd gathered along the way.

Illustration by Mark Viney.

After all, I had one or two wrinkles myself, didn't I? Well, that's what a life of smiling does to people.

Not that it had all been happy-go-lucky. Money troubles were hard to ignore, and goodness knows we'd had our fair share of them, especially when the children were little.

Jerry had hardly missed a day at work, but it had seemed impossible some weeks to make the wages equal the bills. I took in washing and ironing to bring in a bit extra, and I learned to be creative with the food we could afford.

We got by in the end, though, as most of us do. We were together, which was the important thing. We both pulled in the same direction, and we never neglected each other, no matter what else happened.

"I know it's somewhere," Jerry said now, still hunting through his pockets. So far, his search had produced half a packet of mints, an embroidered handkerchief which he never used because it was "far too nice for sneezes", three buttons, fifty-eight pence and a small collection of fluff.

114

Ring

by Lily Garth.

"If you find another two pence," I said, "that will make sixty, so we can call that my anniversary present."

He tilted his head up at me.

"You know it has to be a ring. It's always a ring, that's the rule."

I knew. A ring for every anniversary, that was our special tradition. I would have looked very strange if I had enough fingers for every one he'd given me. Usually, I only wore my engagement and wedding rings — both of them worn thin over the years and neither of them made of real precious metal in the first place. It was a wonder they'd survived this long, but they had. I supposed it just proved that things didn't have to be expensive to last. Of course, I'd known that all along.

I kept the rest of the rings in a box that Jerry carved for me from an old cherry tree which he was paid to cut down in a rich man's garden. Jerry didn't like cutting down trees. He worried that it hurt them, he said, and wondered where their spirits went.

115

"And even if they don't have spirits," he said, "it still doesn't seem right to do it. Trees ought to be treasured."

Well, we couldn't save the cherry tree, but we could treasure the box. I lined it with a piece of pink velvet curtain that I bought at a jumble sale, thinking somehow that the pink could act as a tribute to all the blossom that never had a chance to bloom. I was always sentimental. We both were.

We'd been married nearly five years when Jerry made me that box. Before then, I'd just kept the rings in a old sweet jar. I couldn't keep them in their boxes because Jerry re-used the same ring box every year. You see, most of the rings didn't come from jeweller's shops.

TRADITIONALLY, a first wedding anniversary is celebrated with paper. Well, that had been easy enough. The young Jerry, down on one knee, had presented me with a paper ring made from a strip of that morning's newspaper, with the date clearly showing.

The second year was marked by cotton, so he used a thread from the inside pocket of his wedding suit (well, his *only* suit) to fashion a ring-sized loop. This pattern continued with many feats of imagination each year until the fifteenth, when the tradition jumped to five-year milestones instead of annual ones.

Jerry wasn't pleased about that.

"I'm not waiting five years between gifts," he said. "Each year together is important. We'll just have to make up our own rule."

So we did. We took inspiration from the symbols that already existed. For example, the eighth anniversary had been salt, and Jerry had glued rock salt crystals together in a lovely, if somewhat lumpy circle. On our eighteenth, he did the same with peppercorns.

Oh, we'd had some fun along the way, and one or two mishaps, too. The thirty-second was particularly memorable. We decided on chocolate, and as Jerry was no whiz in the kitchen, I had to make the ring that year. It must have been several dozen delicious versions later before I managed to create a white and milk marbled ring with a dark chocolate jewel.

When it came to the expensive anniversaries, we had hoped to be able to afford the real things — the pearl, the ruby, the sapphire — but it was not to be. The pearl was carved from a discarded oyster shell we found on a Kent beach on a rare weekend's holiday. The ruby was a huge fake ring from a ten-pence gumball machine. The sapphire was blue glass from an old bottle, fixed on to a piece of old wiring.

We were never rich. We did mind about being poor sometimes, but our family was healthy and you can't buy something that valuable, can you? So, shoes were patched and so were gutters ("hoofs and roofs", as we used to say), and we managed.

Our three children grew up and got jobs and left home one by one. We did our best to give each of them a helping hand, by saving on bits and pieces here and there. And then, of course, the grandchildren came along and it gave us such pleasure to buy them things that it made up for all the scrimping and the extra hours of work we'd done over the years.

O N the morning of our golden anniversary, Jerry was upset because he had planned to buy me a real gold ring, but the oven had broken and we had to pay to have it repaired. Our eldest daughter knew about this, and she said she'd take us out for a pub lunch to cheer us up. All the family were there, so we couldn't help enjoying ourselves.

But the big surprise came afterwards. Melanie insisted that we walk home a different way through the park, and as we came through the trees, we saw a small patch of buttercups.

"It's just like the hymn, 'Daisies are our silver, buttercups our gold. These are all the treasures we can have or hold'." Jerry chuckled as he wove the buttercup stems into a gold ring. "If only I'd thought of this when we needed silver," he joked, "I wouldn't have had to waste that tin foil!"

So here we were now, on our diamond anniversary, with Jerry kneeling as he always did, finally finding the ring box and holding it up to me. This annual moment meant so much to us both. We'd been through so much together, so many happy times, so many difficult things, and we were still daft and romantic enough to do this.

"Sixty years!" Jerry said, laughing. "How lucky are we?"

"Very lucky," I answered. Thanking him, with tears in my eyes, I accepted the ring box. Just before I opened it, I had the funniest feeling that something was different. My heart leapt. Suddenly, I believed that this year, by some miracle, we truly were rich and that the box would contain a real diamond ring.

Shaking with anticipation, I pulled off the lid. I caught my breath.

It shone. It sparkled. It was beautiful. Our diamond!

"It's not real, of course," Jerry said. "Just a pretty glass bauble."

Immediately shocked and ashamed, I smiled and shook my head. Of course it wasn't a real diamond. Behind Jerry, I could see the unpaid gas bill on the mantelpiece. How did I ever think that we could afford a genuine diamond? What a silly extravagance that would have been. And yet . . .

The magazines and movies were full of wealthy, glamorous celebrities, dripping with jewels, weren't they? How lucky they all seemed — and how jealous I felt sometimes.

But only for a moment — because I knew I was being silly. Why should I envy such a lifestyle, when there in front of me, gazing adoringly at me as he had done for more than sixty years, was my dear husband, my one and only true love? There was nothing to be jealous of. The diamond might not be real, but the love was, the marriage was.

After helping Jerry to his feet, I kissed him. Who could tell — maybe one day some of those movie stars would be as rich and as lucky as we were. ■

When Emma Came To Stay

AS I watch Bethany fix her sister's wedding veil, warmth spreads through my heart. Their closeness is so wonderful to see.

Downstairs, my husband, John, is busy rehearsing his speech, with Jason listening patiently for the hundredth time.

This house is alive with love and laughter today, a very special day when the happy ending that I prayed for has come true.

That thundery night over ten years ago seems like a lifetime away now. I'm so proud watching Emma prepare for her big day, happy and confident — a million miles away from that scared thirteen-year-old who walked into our lives during a storm . . .

Soon she'll walk down the aisle with Matthew, her very own Prince Charming, and the second half of her fairytale will have begun.

Illustration by Bianchi.

The years have flown and it seems like only yesterday that I realised I could never give Emma up . . .

✳   ✳   ✳   ✳

We'd been fostering for over fifteen years, John and I, so it wasn't as if we were novices. We did understand there comes a time to let go, and say goodbye, once you've done the best you can for the fragile cargo you've been entrusted with, someone else's child.

It's hard to let go when you've grown to love someone, but if foster parents don't accept that, they're heading for heartache. Besides, there's nothing better than seeing parent and child together again, just as they should be.

We'd been lucky; a good marriage, two wonderful kids and a house full to

by Hilary Halliwell.

bursting with love and laughter over the years. Enough happy memories to last a lifetime, born here in our ordinary semi-detached house.

Birthday parties in the garden with John doing his magic tricks, and me in charge of the lucky dip. Christmases filled with joy, love and paper-chains.

Last but not least, our annual holiday to Skegness, our old caravan and a little rented beach-hut at good old Skeggy. Sometimes six or seven of us, and the dog, crammed in, rain or shine. Absolute heaven!

We've fostered lots of children, and still have contact with most of them. It's lovely to see them making a go of their lives, sometimes against all the odds. But this day is more than I ever dared hope for . . .

EMMA smiles a radiant smile; she's beautiful, more so than ever today. I take her hand, my eyes saying it all.

"Thanks, Mum, thanks for all this," she says. "I love you and Dad so much, you know . . ."

"Of course we know." I swallow the lump in my throat. No sadness today, simply joy. That day all those years ago, this would have seemed impossible . . .

John and I had more or less decided to scale down the amount of fostering we did. We'd take the short-stay children, we thought — after all, we weren't getting any younger. Perhaps it was time to do some of the things that we'd

119

put on hold, before we got too old to be daring.

Then came a frantic phone call from Cathy, our foster-team contact. A child in dire need. How could I say no?

I never get used to hearing what some children go through, and this little girl was a tragic case. Every child is precious in my book, but sadly, this isn't a perfect world.

"She's had a rough time. I'd better warn you, she has her problems, Joan. I wouldn't ask you, but . . ."

I'd heard it all before, of course.

"When can we expect her?"

John looked at me, aghast, from across the sitting-room.

"Come on, Joan, I thought we agreed — no more long-term?"

The trouble is, once I know the child's name it forms this invisible bond.

"She's called Emma. And she needs us."

I'm glad to say he doesn't take much persuading, John, not when it comes to a child in need. That's what I love about him.

EMMA arrived in a thunderstorm. A pretty girl, with marmalade hair and a temper to match if her expression was anything to go by! She trusted no-one.

"Hello, Emma. Come on in. My name's Joan, and this is my husband, John. What an awful night!

"I'll show you up to your room, while John puts the kettle on . . ." I smiled at her, but her face was blank. She'd shut out the world.

"Hot chocolate or cocoa, Emma?" John asked in his easy way. But Emma blanked him. Head down, she started up the stairs behind me.

"Do I have to share a room?" she asked gruffly.

"No, this is your room, love. You can put your own posters up, make it just like you want it."

"I'm not staying. Well, not long, anyway . . ." She scowled at me, and curled her lip as she looked about.

Thirteen going on forty! Suspicion, anger, it was all there in her young eyes for anyone who took the time to look. I wanted to weep, but you can't do that in front of a child.

"Sorry about the football posters," I said as I helped her unpack her meagre belongings. "You can change those in the morning if you want. We could go into town, get you some better ones. I can't keep up with who's in and who's out, since Beth left home."

John had made her a cup of hot chocolate as I continued trying to ease the tension that hung in the house like a fog.

I left with a cheery goodnight that got no response at all. Her quiet little sobs followed me to my bed. I knew I had to give her space, but it's so hard when all you want to do is make everything right.

I didn't sleep much that night. In the wee small hours I crept to her room and listened, hoping against hope that she'd drifted off to a better place in her dreams.

I N the early hours, I found myself sitting at the kitchen table nursing a mug of cold tea. Hearing about a case like Emma's is something I've never got used to, though you'd have thought I'd have heard it all.

"Can I have a drink?"

Her voice made me jump. She stood in the doorway, her face sullen, her eyes so much older than her tender years.

I put her drink next to where I sat.

"Come and sit down." I tapped the seat next to me. "Tell me all about what you like to do. I could do with some company!"

Still silence. Then a flash of lightning sent her running to me. She sat down, still careful not to have any physical contact.

"I don't like lightning, either." I edged her drink towards her, and she gulped at it, eyes wide with fear.

"Got any biscuits?" Her voice was flat, emotionless.

I looked at her thin little figure. She looked world-weary, yet I could see she was very pretty.

I got the biscuit tin down and put it in front of her. If biscuits would make her feel better, then biscuits she would have.

She dived in, ravenous, and at that moment, I felt a bond form, as strong as when I'd seen my own children arrive in this world. Like them, Emma was so vulnerable, and completely dependent on me!

My heart went out to her. I wanted to wrap her in my arms and chase all her nightmares away. I felt as if my heart would break before the dawn did, that stormy day.

*　　*　　*　　*

Over the next few days, with gentle coaxing and a certain amount of leaving her to her own devices, Emma began to settle. It was painfully slow, but John has this wonderful way of knowing when to back off, so I followed his lead.

"How about a game of cards, Joan? Emma? Or a board game. We've got loads, and I'm really easy to beat!" John heaved a pile of them out of the dresser cupboard.

"I'm going to bed." And without a backward glance, she went upstairs.

"Emma, it's only five o'clock!" I called after her. "You've had no supper yet and it's burgers tonight!"

She paused.

"McDonald's or Burger King?"

"You wait till you taste Joan Burgers. Knock spots off them fast food

121

places, and her chips, well . . ."

But Emma was having absolutely none of it. She disappeared round the turn of the stairs, and her voice floated back.

"No, thanks. I only like proper burgers!"

"Come down and have your tea, Emma!" I called, but John put his arm around me.

"Let her go, love. It's early days . . . I'll have hers!" His joke made me smile. Of course, he was right.

John was on his second burger and I sat unable to eat a single chip when the door opened and Emma came in.

I went over to the stove and put some leftover chips and a burger on a plate.

"Here, take yours upstairs if you like."

I put the plate down on the work surface, sat down and made myself eat.

Still nothing! Getting a drink, she turned to go back upstairs, but then, quite suddenly, she stopped, reached out, and took the plate with her.

I felt a sigh of relief rise in me. I couldn't bear to think of her hungry.

From then on, slowly, I saw her start to respond. And then Brandy took a hand.

Brandy, like Emma, was wished upon us, but unlike Emma, he'd walked out of the cat basket as if he already owned the place.

The "Friend" Remembers Wartime Chanteuses & Entertainers

Anne Shelton OBE 1923 — 1994

ANNE SHELTON was born in Dulwich, South London, and became one of Britain's best-loved popular singers.

Anne frequently entertained the troops during World War II and starred in the "Forces' Sweetheart" radio show. She was a real beauty, with thick, red-gold hair and blue eyes, and received hundreds of letters each week from the boys in khaki and blue.

Are you as lovely as your voice? one read.

Like Vera Lynn, she sang with the popular Albert Ambrose Orchestra and was even given a regular spot on one of his radio shows when she was only sixteen.

Her own radio show, "Introducing Anne", became popular amongst the troops. Originally devised for soldiers serving in the North African desert, it ran for over four years.

Anne adopted "Lili Marlene" as a signature piece; English lyrics were added by Tommy Connor and her recording was released in 1944. It was an immediate success. She went on to record a string of massive-selling hits, including "My Yiddishe Momme", "Begin The Beguine" and "Lay Down Your Arms", which reached the top of the charts in 1956.

On the occasions that Glenn Miller visited Britain, she regularly appeared with his band. Miller claimed she had a "pure gold voice".

She was in constant demand by the early Forties and appeared in numerous films such as "King Arthur Was A Gentleman" (1942) and "Bees In Paradise" (1944).

122

Anne Shelton

After the war, Anne toured extensively. She made countless guest appearances and worked with many variety performers.

Anne was the first British artist to cover the entire United States with a tour that lasted a year. She even topped the bill at New York's Copacabana.

In 1990 she was appointed OBE for services to the Not Forgotten Association — a charity that provides care and support for disabled ex-service personnel.

The neighbour who had been desperate to re-home him laughed.

"Looks like he knows who's in charge, Joan!"

I've never seen a small ginger kitten with more sense of his own importance. Brandy was a laugh a minute, and of course, Emma could hardly ignore him.

Time and time again I'd catch her stroking him as he sat in the kitchen by the stove. I never drew attention to it, though. Perhaps the kitten's winning ways would help more than John and I ever could.

The first time our Beth came home to visit was a nightmare.

"Hi, Emma!" Bethany dropped her stuff and grinned at her.

"Bethany's going to be a vet!" I said, trying to break the ice. The look Emma gave Beth did nothing for family harmony, I can tell you.

"What do you want to be when you leave school?" I asked, trying to include Emma.

"Not a stupid vet."

And that was more or less the last we saw of her, except at mealtimes, till Bethany left. At least she'd got over her reluctance to eat. I was grateful for small mercies.

Beth isn't one to give up. On the Sunday, I actually heard them talking in Beth's room. I admit I eavesdropped.

"How do you do that line round your eyes? Did it hurt when you had your

123

belly button pierced?" Emma's voice was eager.

I'd hated Beth's piercing until that moment, but now I was so glad she'd had it done.

"Do you want me to show you how to do your eyes, Em? You can have this pencil — but don't tell Mum I gave it to you!"

There was a sudden unified giggling, wonderful to hear.

From that moment, things improved. Emma started to relax, and never more so than when Beth came at weekends.

Little by little, Brandy became Emma's cat. The day she accepted my suggestion she might like to give him his dinner, I had to walk out of the kitchen. I couldn't see her opening the tin of kitten food for tears.

Not long after that, the next breakthrough happened, and you could have knocked me over with a feather . . .

"I'm off for a walk. Anyone fancy coming?" John said, one evening. I was just about to say no, because Emma and I were watching this animal show, when Emma looked up.

"I'll come! If it's OK?" She looked at me, her face questioning.

"'Course, love. Think I'll stay, though. I'll tape the show for you two if you like."

I watched from behind the curtains as they made their way up the street, looking like any normal father and daughter.

Such a simple thing, but it meant the world to me seeing Emma being a child — even if she did have a bit too much eye-liner on.

Over the next few weeks we began to see a happy young girl emerging. Worth all the fancy holidays in the world to us; I felt as if I'd won the lottery.

Emma, with her marmalade hair and vivid blue eyes, had learned to smile, to giggle and to trust a little. Gradually, she let us into her world.

The short stay turned into weeks, then into months.

Oh, I won't say it was all plain sailing. Just as you thought you were getting there, up would go the shutters again.

It was a roller-coaster, even for us with all our years of experience. Nothing had prepared us for Emma.

Like the day I couldn't find my purse . . .

EMMA had settled in at school. She'd come on so well, to be honest, I was really hopeful we were over the worst.

"Have you see my purse, John? I can't find it anywhere . . ."

"No, where did you last have it?" he replied.

I'd given Emma some lunch money moments before. She'd asked for extra for sweets, but I'd no more change.

"You can have some tonight, love!" I'd said.

"OK."

And that had been that.

It niggled me all day. I'd wrecked the house looking for it, but nothing! When she got home, I thought she might have seen what I'd done with the blessed thing.

"You haven't seen my purse, Emma, have you?"

Her face had darkened, her eyes fearful. I wanted to bite my tongue off; she thought I was accusing her!

She sank to the floor, curling herself up small, visibly shaking.

"I didn't take it! Honestly! Don't send me away . . ."

When John went to comfort her, she'd flinched, putting up her arms as if to protect herself.

I got down on the floor and held her and John held us both, and there the three of us sat, huddled together in a heap. I never wanted to let go of her again.

Yes, that was the moment I knew.

"We didn't think you'd take it, love, we just wondered if you'd seen it! Anyway, we're not going to send you away over a silly purse, or anything else."

Gradually her body relaxed, and she looked at me with eyes that for the first time were the eyes of a child.

I found the wretched purse next morning — in the bread bin of all places!

"A RE there any relatives?" I asked Cathy at our regular meeting a few days later.

"No. The surviving grandparents are living abroad and, frankly, just not interested."

I sighed in disbelief.

"And the mother's sister wants nothing more to do with any of the family."

I sat there hardly believing what I was hearing.

"So what you're saying is, Emma has no family, and precious little hope of getting one?"

I was heartbroken.

This wasn't me! I accepted that the world was less than perfect. After all, I'd seen more of it than most.

So why, why just as we were thinking that maybe it should be our time, was I getting so involved?

Cathy looked at me and smiled.

"Might it be best for all concerned to move Emma? You've done a wonderful job," she added, gently touching my hand.

Tears were smarting in my eyes.

"No way! Take away the little trust and stability she's built up?" I gazed at her.

"You said that the next move was adoption? We'll adopt her! Why put her through yet another move?"

John and I had only touched on the subject, but in my heart I knew he'd already made up his mind, Emma was here to stay.

Cathy drew back a little.

"Think carefully about it, Joan. Talk to John and the children, see how they feel; it affects you all, you know! Meanwhile, I'll make some discreet enquiries at my end, talk to the adoption team."

When Cathy left, I sat on looking out into the garden.

The kitten was trying to catch a "butterfly" made of paper on the end of some string. John was urging Brandy to jump higher, and as I heard Emma laugh, I saw happiness where previously I'd seen only despair.

That weekend, we got everyone down to visit, including John's mum and my mum and dad. While Emma got to know the grandparents, we talked to Beth, and so on round the family.

Their response was what I expected.

"Oh, Mum, she'll be so made up!" Beth was excited. "Em said just the other week how she wished she never had to leave! And a younger sister? Just what I always wanted."

It was a bit more complicated when we asked Jason. I really wasn't sure how he'd react to being permanently outnumbered by two sisters.

"Cool! When's lunch, then?"

Our parents were unanimous, and only wondered what had taken us so long.

THAT evening after everyone had left, we three sat at the table where she and I had sat that first morning.

"Emma, it must be a bit quiet here with us two old fogies. Are you sure you're happy?"

Emma didn't answer, but her tears did!

"What's all this now?" John leaned to put his arm round her shoulders.

"Don't send me away!" She sobbed. "You can't send me away!"

I will never forget the look on her face.

"Send you away? Of course not, Emma! Why would we? That was the last thing we want!"

I hugged her.

"Look, we just want to know how you feel about staying on here permanently — becoming our real daughter?"

She looked up, stunned, her eyes full of love.

"Like to be adopted? Wow, cool!" A little smile arrived, even as the remains of a sob were audible.

Brandy crossed the kitchen floor and jumped up on to her lap, and we fell into a joyous cuddle together, the four of us.

"I'll stay here with you for ever and ever!"

As she clung to us, I could feel the hurt in her young heart start to ebb away. Yes, there were still tears, but now they were tears of joy, of hope, of healing.

In the weeks and months that followed we watched Emma blossom. She knew at long last she was truly loved, and that was all she ever needed.

SO here we are, ten years down the line, our lives transformed. We never made it up the Amazon, nor did we go whitewater rafting, but we went back to Skeggy for the next ten years or so. That's where Emma met her Matthew, three years ago.

Today they'll wake up the aisle together, and I'm the proudest mum on the planet.

We've had three weddings in as many years. First Jason married his Jenny, a lovely Welsh girl, a farmer's daughter.

Then Beth married Steve, whom she met at vet school. They made us grandparents last year.

Now it's Emma's turn.

I take a small box from the dressing-table drawer. Something old — the pearl necklace my mother gave me when John and I were wed. Beth had the matching bracelet when she married, and Jenny the earrings. I've kept the ring myself.

Pearls are for tears, they say, but tears aren't always for sorrow, are they?

I hand Emma the box.

"Something old for you, my darling . . ." And I smile.

"Oh, Mum, it's lovely. Thank you!" The three of us hug, a mother and her two beautiful daughters together on this special day.

John's hand is in mine as Emma and Matthew walk past up the aisle, a married couple, she smiles at me, eyes brimming with love.

Yes, pearls can bring tears of happiness, too. And I'm living proof of that. ■

New Beginnings

AS Peg watched the happy couples alighting from the air-conditioned coach into the warmth of the afternoon sun, she became painfully aware that she was the only person sitting alone. Hearing each couple's laughter as they carried their cases into the brightly painted apartment blocks nestling close to the blue sea, she wondered yet again whether this sudden decision to get away for a few days had been such a good idea after all.

She remembered the carefree way she had told her partner in the travel agency what she was planning.

Illustration by Ben Warner.

by Joy Harvey.

"Well, that's the end of the summer rush and the last-minute people so, if you don't mind, Shirley, I'm going off to Cyprus again for a few days in the sun."

"Good idea, Peg," Shirley had replied cheerfully. "George and I aren't going away until the end of this month, so it's an ideal time."

When the coach reached her stop, the driver pulled her one small suitcase from the luggage compartment and closed the panel. As he drove quickly away, she felt even more alone.

Peg's feelings of doubt subsided as she heard her name being called excitedly from the entrance to the small apartment building.

"Mrs Peg, Mrs Peg, I'm so happy to see you again. Welcome, welcome."

She looked up to see Costa, long grey hair flowing behind him, racing down the steps towards her at a speed that would frighten many men half his age.

He hugged her, kissed her on both cheeks, picked up her case and led her up the steps into the cool reception lounge where his smiling wife repeated the enthusiastic greeting.

"Fortunately, we are not quite full, Mrs Peg, so we were able to keep your favourite apartment empty, just in case."

The warmth of the welcome instantly drove all doubts from Peg's mind. Of course she had been right to come back here for a few days. Nowhere else in the world did she have friends who always greeted her this warmly, who devoted their time to her happiness and then cried so openly when she had to leave.

Peg walked slowly and thoughtfully up the two flights of stairs to her apartment, suddenly feeling a brief twinge of envy as a giggling young couple clutching beach towels and smelling of suntan oil passed her hurriedly.

As she entered her familiar apartment, she smiled as she saw the unfastened straps on her case. Of course, everything had been unpacked and put away neatly.

Opening the door of the small fridge, she knew that she would find a carton of milk, a bottle of cold water and a bottle of her favourite white wine. Turning her head quickly to the shelf beside the small kitchen sink, she smiled. As always, there was the corkscrew . . . and two glasses.

There were always two glasses on that shelf, but Peg had always chosen to use only one in all her visits during these last four years.

She kept telling herself that one day she would need that second glass — but not yet, not until she felt better about herself and had learned to trust again.

Peg awoke slowly the next morning and listened to the small waves lapping gently on the sand, the same sound that had lulled her to sleep the night before.

AFTER a light breakfast, she walked across the beach to the only vacant sun umbrella, which covered two beach beds, and checked the tag on it bearing her apartment number.

This umbrella was going to be an essential part of her first day or two, because she burned easily in the hot sun.

Walking out through the warm shallow water, Peg swam strongly along to the point and back again. This was always her favourite start to a day here, a part of the pattern that she had established during these past four years.

As she walked back across the hot sand towards her beach umbrella, the sight of a man sitting on the edge of one her sunbeds irritated her. He saw her approaching and stood, tall and lean, awkwardly cramped under the umbrella frame.

He spoke first, obviously anxious to reassure her.

"Good morning. I must apologise for this intrusion, but the umbrella allocated to me has been taken."

130

He pointed to where an elderly couple lay on sunbeds, and Peg noticed the pair of crutches under one of the beds.

"There were no others available so I took the liberty of sheltering here because . . ." he looked down briefly at his very white skin ". . . the sun is quite a bit stronger than I expected. I do hope you don't mind."

PEG smiled sympathetically at this formal explanation from someone who was definitely not used to trying to stand under a rather low beach umbrella.

"Please sit down. This shade has been adjusted for my height, not yours."

She sat on her sunbed facing him.

"Please feel free to shelter here any time. Actually, I'm seldom here because I like to swim or just walk along the sand most of the time."

She quickly towelled her short bobbed hair.

"Back home, I work in a busy office, so I need to come here at least twice a year for peace, relaxation and sheer laziness."

The man seemed to have partly recovered his composure as Peg spoke and appeared almost relieved by the reasons she gave for her visits here.

He introduced himself as Bob and explained that he had come to Cyprus for a business meeting, but it had suddenly been postponed for three days.

"So I thought that I would take the opportunity for a much-needed break. I have to travel frequently at very short notice, but I never seem to get time to see anything of the places I visit."

He became aware that Peg was staring at him, her brow furrowed in thought.

"What's wrong?" he asked gently. "What did I say?"

"It's not what you said, Bob, it's your voice, the way you speak. I've heard it before somewhere, often. Tell me, are you on the radio or something?"

Bob laughed.

"Goodness me, no. The funny thing is that I was going to ask you the very same question. Your choice of expressions, your tone — it's all strangely familiar.

"As for me being on the radio, my job is far less glamorous. I work for a large company and have to keep a suitcase packed for short-notice trips to Europe. Fortunately, there is a very helpful travel agency locally and Margaret, the lady there, always manages to find me a flight somehow within a few hours. I really don't know what I would do without her —"

He stopped speaking and studied her face.

"Now what have I said, Peg? You've got that look again."

She didn't answer him, but her look of curiosity slowly changed to one of amusement, before she burst into peals of laughter.

Bob stood up in alarm.

"What's wrong, Peg? Do you have the hiccups? Shall I get you a glass of water?"

Unable to reply, Peg gestured at him to sit down again before she eventually controlled her laughter.

"There's nothing wrong — *Bob*. I haven't got the hiccups — *Robert*. And I don't need a glass of water — *Mr Grayling*."

Bob's look of complete bewilderment lasted only a few seconds.

"Of course," he said. "That's why your voice was so familiar. Yes . . . Peg . . . Margaret . . . *the travel agency!* If we'd been speaking on the phone I would have known you immediately."

FOR the remainder of that day they were like long-lost friends reunited, each relaxing as it became obvious that neither was looking for a whirlwind holiday romance.

For dinner that evening at a beach taverna, they shared a leisurely *meze* meal of almost twenty small dishes of spicy Cypriot foods that the owner brought more slowly than usual, sensing that their softly spoken non-stop conversation was just as important to them as the food.

Their conversation quickly flowed from amusing memories of Peg's clever solutions to Bob's travel problems on to brief explanations of their present lifestyles.

Peg could not help laughing at Bob's deliberately light-hearted account of how his wife left him for a handsome smooth-talker who gave her a wonderful and adventurous life until all her money was gone.

"Then," Bob said, "he was gone, too."

Peg stated simply that her husband had walked away from his family four years ago, without explanation.

Their twin boys still lived with her at home and had now almost completed their education.

"We don't go on holiday together any more," Peg said with a wry smile. "The boys told me last year, kindly but firmly, that they still wanted to have fun but I kept choosing 'rocking-chair' holidays."

During the slow walk back to their neighbouring apartment blocks, their light-hearted conversation became punctuated by short silences and awkwardly polite replies to innocent remarks. Peg realised that she was feeling the same fluttering of nervousness and anxiety about how to say goodnight that she had felt on her very first date, all those years ago.

Glancing furtively at Bob's face, she sensed that he, too, was having the same uncomfortable teenage-type worries, hoping desperately not to spoil this new friendship.

As they reached the foot of the steps to her block. Peg was painfully aware that her hands felt damp and her breathing was much too fast, but Bob gently took both her hands and turned her so that her back was towards the lights of the building. He leaned forward, kissed her lightly on both cheeks, moved back slightly and thanked her warmly for making his day so enjoyable.

Peg realised that he had deliberately turned her face into shadow to hide her possible embarrassment and she instinctively squeezed his hands in gratitude.

Bob's quick smile clearly showed his understanding. Then he released her hands, waved towards the sea and spoke cheerfully.

"See you tomorrow, Peg?"

AS she closed her apartment door behind her, Peg realised that there was no way she could get to sleep just yet. Remembering the bottle of wine in the fridge, she poured a glass and sat in one of the comfortable armchairs to relax and review the day's events.

Smiling to herself, she fetched the second glass and placed it gently on the table in front of the empty chair opposite her.

The next two days passed far too quickly as they swam together, walked along the edge of the water or just talked in the shade. Each felt much more relaxed after the awkwardness of their first goodnight, and even that had only progressed to a hug and a quick brushing of lips.

"When you get home, Peg, may I phone you?" Bob asked, a little nervously, as they parted on the evening of his last day. "Not about flights, I mean . . . just . . ."

Peg hugged him fiercely and kissed his cheek.

"Of course you can. If you hadn't asked, I would have called you."

They both laughed with relief at this open admission of their own inner feelings and hugged each other warmly. As they parted with a cheerful wave after three days together, each felt the same sudden chill of loneliness.

Two days later, as Peg waited for her coach back to the airport, she kept toying with the small cardboard box that she would not put down.

She had asked Costa that morning if she could buy the two glasses from her apartment to take home. He had looked puzzled, but instantly told her she could have them for free and agreed to pack them carefully for her. She explained to him she had always been touched by the way that there had been two glasses every time she had stayed with them, but she had only ever needed one.

"But now, Costa, I hope that I will need them both before I come here again." ■

by Teresa
Ashby.

Illustration by Richard Eraut.

The Secret Recipe

M UCH was made of Grandma's secret recipe in our family. It was
said to have been passed down from generation to generation,
with everyone adding a little something of their own to the
ingredients.

From the time I was a little girl, small enough to sit on Grandma's lap while
she read me stories from an old dusty book of my mother's, she'd told me
about the recipe.

Well, no, that's not right. She actually told me about the women who had
contributed to it. She told me about her mother who had worked for the
French Resistance, and her grandmother who had run away to Australia and
married the owner of an opal mine.

134

She'd made a fortune and spent it again by the time she and her husband returned to start their family.

She told me of her great-grandmother who had gone across the Atlantic on board a ship from Ireland with eight of her twelve children and, within two years, had come back again.

And the great-grandmother's mother, who had run away from home at the age of ten and gone to work for a real earl on a big estate.

The rest she left to my imagination.

You wouldn't think all those ladies had time for recipes, would you? I imagined my great-grandmother baking secret buns in a French kitchen while German boots marched past, and the Australian grandmother cooking up something on an open fire outside her mine.

As for the Irish one, did she elbow the cook out of the ship's galley and commandeer his stove? Or did she cook on an open fire on the deck? She might have set the sails on fire!

The little girl who ran away to go into service became a great cook. She was an exhibition cook, my grandma said, who travelled all over the world giving demonstrations of her skills.

W HAT did you do, Grandma?" I used to ask her. "What exciting adventures did you have?"

"Why, darling, I was a spy in Russia in the days of the iron curtain," she told me. "I used to wear white fur and communicate with other spies in complicated codes. I even had a tiny camera which I hid under my hat."

"Did you know James Bond?" I asked.

"Of course not." She sniffed. "He's a fictional character."

My mother said the most exciting thing she ever did was marry my father and have me.

She also hinted that Grandma's stories of being a spy might be a bit exaggerated, although she admitted that Grandma did go to Moscow once with an orchestra.

Personally, I never doubted Grandma. Anything she said was good enough for me.

I often asked Grandma what her secret recipe was and she'd always tap the side of her nose.

"If I told you, it wouldn't be much of a secret, would it?" she'd say.

I tried to guess. I strongly suspected that it was her melt-in-the-mouth scones, but it could just as easily have been her light and fluffy pancakes, or even her cinnamon apple cake.

It's funny because I never saw her use a recipe when she was baking. She didn't even own a set of scales and would toss all her ingredients into a huge china mixing bowl and produce all kinds of wonders.

And, lucky me, I always got to lick the spoon.

AS I grew up, Grandma's secret recipe was mentioned less and less. I thought she might give it to me on my wedding day and I whispered as much in her ear as she hugged me after the ceremony.

"You're not ready yet," she whispered back. "You will have it when the time is right. I'm glad you've not forgotten about it, though."

But I was impatient. I wanted to try the recipe on my new husband. I wanted to impress him with a cake that had been baked by generations before me.

I wanted to produce the recipe at a dinner for my husband's boss and help him gain the promotion he so richly deserved.

"What is it?" I asked my mum several months later as I sat in her kitchen eating butterfly buns. "You don't even make the same things as Grandma. So what is the recipe?"

"You'll find out," she told me mysteriously. "All in good time."

"Oh, Mother," I groaned.

"Patience is a virtue," Mum said, pouring me another cup of tea.

I found myself growing more curious, the way you do when something appears to be forbidden.

✳   ✳   ✳   ✳

But then, just after our first wedding anniversary, I had other things to think about. Mum was over the moon and Grandma was head first in the cupboard, sorting through her old knitting patterns.

"I know I've got a whole stack of them here somewhere," her muffled voice drifted out. "You can't have too many matinée jackets and bootees."

"And I'll crochet a shawl," my mum said, her eyes shining with joy.

And I knew it would be something special, too. Mum's incredibly gifted like that.

And Grandma is gifted, too. Give her a pair of knitting needles and some wool and she can work magic. There was nothing you could buy in a shop that came close to my Grandma's exquisite outfits.

As my bump grew, I went shopping with Mum and Grandma. We giggled like teenagers over bright colourful toys and cooed over tiny vests.

We filled bags with baby things and took them home to put in the nursery with the sunny yellow walls and jungle animals.

Grandma tied her wedding ring to a length of white wool and dangled it above my ever-growing bump.

"Definitely a girl," she announced. "No two ways about it. And if I'm right, it'll be time to hand down the recipe, isn't that so, Dawn?"

Mum nodded her agreement.

I felt a tingle of excitement, as if I were about to be allowed into an exclusive club.

AND a week later, I was sitting up in my hospital bed with my new daughter sleeping in a cot at my side.

"Welcome, Amy," Grandma said, and my little one's eyes fluttered open. She looked at Grandma as if she knew her well.

"May I hold her, Della?"

"Of course," I said. I would have been disappointed if she hadn't wanted to hold her first great-grandchild.

She sat in the nursing chair beside the bed and Mum placed baby Amy in her arms. Grandma's tears of happiness dripped on the beautiful shawl Mum had made.

Then Mum began to unload her bulging bag.

"Mrs Oakley from the corner sent you this and the Italian people from the greengrocer's asked me to give you this . . ."

She unpacked envelopes and parcels from people I barely knew as Grandma watched.

"Never mind all that. Give her the recipe, Dawn," Grandma said. "Give her the recipe."

Smiling, Mum took an envelope from her bag.

"It's in there," she said. "And it's yours now."

I held it for a moment, almost too scared to open it. What if I was disappointed? What if I couldn't do justice to the recipe?

Grandma and Mum looked impatient as I opened the envelope carefully.

The envelope contained several pieces of paper in various sizes and colours. Some were just little scraps, others fancy, embossed writing paper.

"Every generation writes their ingredients for a happy life," Grandma explained. "You will add your own one day and pass it on to Amy when you feel the time is right."

Always fight for what you know is right, Grandma's mother, who had been in the French Resistance, had written. *Live for the moment, remember to smile often and cry rarely.*

Seize the moment, the Australian grandmother had advised. *Make time to sit in the sun and listen to the birds. Make time to live.*

The grandmother who had travelled across the Atlantic had written in a sweeping hand, *Never be afraid to take a step into the unknown. But be ready to take a step backwards if needs be.*

And the one who had run away to work for an earl said, *A better life is there if you look for it. And if you don't, then you don't want it. Sometimes the apples with the most scars are the most flavoursome.* She'd added a recipe for apple cake (*guaranteed to make the children and the menfolk happy!*)

Grandma had written, on a small square of violet notepaper, *To be blessed with a vivid imagination can be a curse or a gift — how you use it is up to you.*

And Mum had used a small piece of pink card for her quote.

You have an endless supply of patience and you need never run out. Be a mother to your daughter when she is small and she will one day be a friend to you.

"IMAGINATION, Grandma?" I said with a smile. "Aren't the stories you told me true?"

She smiled back, but then gazed down blissfully at my newborn daughter, not giving me an answer.

I didn't really want an answer anyway. I liked to think some of her stories had a basis in the truth.

She'd always made up wonderful stories and I will remember them for ever and tell them to my own grandchildren one day.

I reached out and squeezed Mum's hand. To think that when I was younger, I used to get cross with her for not being like my best friend Sal's mum.

Sal's mum had a trendy hairstyle and borrowed Sal's clothes. I thought she was cool. But Sal's mum is still wearing clothes meant for a teenager and she's not interested in being a grandmother.

Not like my mum. My friend. My best friend.

I still have a long time to think about what piece of advice I would like to pass on to Amy, but in the meantime, I'm trying to follow the advice contained in the envelope.

I have made the apple cake, though. I made it with scarred, ugly apples and, do you know, it was the most delicious apple cake I've ever tasted! ■

Time For Love

I N one sudden convulsive movement Nat opened his eyes — and groaned. The headache seemed to rise from his shoulders, hit the bones behind his ears and then strike with a hammer blow at his temples. After several seconds he forced himself to turn his eyes towards the window. The light was very bright. He closed his eyes again.

He wasn't normally like this. As far as he remembered, he'd only had a couple of drinks.

He managed a wry grin. It

by
Valerie
Edwards.

*Illustration by
Heidi Spindler.*

must have been Tony. He'd insisted on him trying some fancy cocktail or other. He might have known — Tony was always mucking about.

He almost hadn't gone to the party anyway. He'd put in so many extra hours at work last week that he hadn't felt like it. If Tony hadn't called round for him, he definitely wouldn't have bothered . . .

Suddenly, despite the pain, he shot bolt upright in bed.

If he hadn't gone he wouldn't have met her. She'd been sitting on her own, looking a bit lost — or shy. He knew the feeling — knew what it was like to want to join in but having to steel yourself to make the effort.

He'd studied her, trying to pluck up his own courage. She was a lovely blonde with dark eyes, he saw as he drew closer. They smiled at each other, then exchanged names.

"I'm Annie," she'd said.

"Oh, I like that. It's my gran's name," he'd replied.

Now, blindly, he groped on the floor for his watch, and squinted down.

Eleven-thirty.

He couldn't have slept that long.

He sat on the edge of the bed, willing himself to feel better. Annie, he thought tenderly. Annie. He'd danced with her, held her close, wished the music could have gone on for ever. He'd hardly believed his luck when he'd asked to see her again and she'd said yes, without hesitation.

Suddenly, the world swam sharply into focus.

TODAY. It was today!

He grinned to himself.

"Three o'clock," she'd said. And then she'd had an idea.

"I'd like to go to the zoo. I haven't been since I was little." Well, neither had he!

He showered, hot then cold, and felt invigorated. It had been a great party. He opened the wardrobe, decided on jeans and a T-shirt and his checked shirt. No, it hadn't, he reminded himself — not if I'm honest. It had been meeting Annie that had made it great.

He went into the kitchen, whistling, and checked his watch with the wall clock. Half-past twelve. There wasn't really time to cook a proper meal — he didn't feel like one anyway — so he'd just have a sandwich. With luck, she'd stay on after the zoo. They could have dinner somewhere.

He frowned as he began slicing cheese and bread, wishing he could remember everything that had happened last night. After their final dance, Annie had gone to talk to a girlfriend, and they'd disappeared in the direction of the bathroom. Shortly afterwards, she'd called that she had a lift home tonight, and would see him tomorrow. Then, she'd added something that he hadn't quite caught because of the noise . . . and was gone.

He took a bite out of his sandwich, shrugging. The important thing was their date. Three o'clock at the zoo. His heart jolted happily. Nothing else mattered. Nothing in the whole wide world. Whistling, he made coffee and carried both plate and cup over to a chair.

He'd walk round the block in a while, just to clear his mind properly. He wanted everything to be perfect. This was going to be the most important meeting of his entire life.

IT would have been, except for one thing.

She didn't turn up.

He waited for nearly an hour, walking up and down the pavement, staring over the railings, peering into the distance, growing more and more despondent. He watched people going through the turnstiles, heard the shouts of children, the muted calls of the animals. Once or twice he thought the elderly man in the ticket booth was looking at him, watching with suspicion.

Finally, he gave up and went home. She could be ill, he told himself. Or someone in her family could have had an accident. Or something. Anything. He knew he didn't believe a word of it. It had all been too good to be true. She'd changed her mind. That was it, pure and simple.

He'd never been a great success with girls. He hadn't got the gift of the gab like Tony. And yet somehow he'd thought Annie was different!

Miserably he picked up the Sunday paper, unfolded it and ran his thumb down the crease.

In an instant, seeing the thick black type above the paragraph at the bottom of the page, he remembered exactly what she'd called back to him.

Don't forget to alter your watch!

"You idiot," he said, aloud. "You stupid idiot."

Spring forward, fall back. That's what they always said. He groaned to himself. Would she believe him? Yes, he thought with relief. Yes, a girl like Annie would.

If he had her phone number . . . He couldn't believe that he hadn't. He must have. She'd given it to him, hadn't she? No, she hadn't.

Wildly, he wondered who would know. He got up and paced the floor. It couldn't just end like this, all because of the wretched British Summer Time or whatever it was called.

Just then, the phone rang.

She was hesitant at first, but he was so elated to hear her voice that he spoke over her words, apologising, explaining, desperate.

"I guessed," she said finally. "But then — well, I wasn't sure." She took a deep breath. "I waited for ages and then plucked up the courage and rang Tony. He's a friend of my brother's."

Tony. Oh, he'd forgive him anything now, Nat thought. Anything.

"Let's start again," he breathed. "A meal, this evening?"

"Yes," she said. And then he heard the echo of laughter bubbling along the wire. "But first, there's just one thing — perhaps it would be an idea to synchronise our watches?" ■

by Barbara Dynes.

Illustration by
David McAllister.

The Day Humphrey Bogart went Missing

WHATEVER happened to the art of queuing, Jennifer asked herself, as she entered her local corner shop. It was packed. Late afternoon — school-out time — was a silly time to come shopping. The mums and children always seemed to out-number the goods!

But Jennifer had run out of cat food and Mr Patel sold just about everything. Besides, she enjoyed watching and listening to people . . .

"Gimme your sweet money and I'll not tell Miss Morris about you know what!" the lad in front of her sneered to a younger boy. "OK, Dumbo?"

Jennifer blinked. Intriguing, that "you-know-what" bit. And why Dumbo?

In her day, "Dumbo", from the Disney film, had meant "big ears". Today it probably meant just dumb. She gazed at the younger lad. He had rather neat ears and appeared quite the opposite of dumb. Clutching his money, he stared defiantly at his "friend".

"No, Sean; no way!" he stated.

Good for you, Dumbo, Jennifer thought. She didn't hold with blackmail.

The little scene in front of her was ringing distant bells. She stared over the heads of harassed mothers and their noisy offspring and was transported back sixty or so years . . .

Illustration by Melvyn Warren-Smith.

TO the sound of the siren's wail, eleven-year-old Jennifer raced through the streets of the little Berkshire town. Her coat flew behind her, her heart hammered like mad and Humphrey Bogart, the fat black cat she was holding, wriggled and hissed.

"Stop it! You didn't want to be left on your own, did you, Humphrey?" she gasped. "There could be bombs! We have to go to Gran's whenever there's a raid and Mum's at work, you know we do!"

Jennifer ran on, past the identical terraced houses. It was daytime and sunny, but there weren't many people about. She felt frightened. Air raid sirens were really scary . . .

At last they reached Gran's house. Jennifer banged the brass knocker hard. Twice, three times . . . Her arms ached from holding Humphrey.

A head popped out from number 142, next door. Oh, no; Mrs Draper!

"Ah, Jennifer! Your gran's out. I told her I'd look after you if there was a raid. Come in, child!"

Jennifer could not move. She wanted to go back home, run away . . . anything, rather than go into the Drapers' house. Bombs were nothing compared with Cain Draper.

He was a bit older than her, had red hair and a stupid grin — and he pinched all her sweet coupons every week. Her clever friend, Doreen, called it blackmail.

Jennifer didn't know what blackmail meant. All she knew was that Cain said if she didn't give him her coupons he would tell everyone about the day she kissed Colin Butts.

But Cain had got it all wrong. She didn't even like Colin Butts! Colin had grabbed her and kissed her, not the other way around.

MRS DRAPER stood there waiting, arms folded over her flowered overall. Jennifer knew she'd have to go in. As she made to step over the squat dividing wall between the two houses her arms slackened — and Humphrey Bogart took one almighty leap to freedom, tearing off back down the road.

"Humphrey!" she yelled, about to sprint after him. But Mrs Draper grabbed her arm and pushed her into the house.

"Best get inside, lovey! He'll be all right — nine lives, they've got, cats!"

Jennifer wanted to cry. Inside the house it was all brown and dreary and there was a stale smell of cabbage. Their sitting-room at home had bright yellow walls. Mum had bought a cheap tin of paint at the market.

"There might be a war on, but we can keep cheerful!" she'd said.

Perhaps Mrs Draper liked sad colours.

"Please, can I go and look for Humphrey?" she pleaded.

"No, he'll be back, lovey!" Mrs Draper said. "You go and join the boys in the cellar — we'll all be safe enough there."

Jennifer reluctantly did as she was told. Cain had already had her sweet ration for this week. Perhaps next week she'd ask Mum to buy her sweets for her, then he wouldn't be able to get hold of the coupons. But he might tell everyone . . .

Down in the cellar, Jennifer blinked rapidly as her eyes tried to adjust to the dimness.

"Oh, blimey, look who it is!" Gordon, Cain's older brother, sneered.

Jennifer frowned. She'd heard that Gordon could be a real bully, even worse than Cain.

Cain, who was sitting on the dusty floor pulling an old wireless apart, looked up, grinning. His face was smudged with grease and his red hair flopped into his eyes, as usual.

"Little Jennifer Gurton! What you doing here?"

"My mum's at work and Gran's out," Jennifer mumbled, looking around. There was a bench and some old chairs and a table covered in books, games, torches and stuff. Stuck on the whitewashed wall was a big picture of footballers and Jennifer stood staring at Stanley Matthews' knees, praying the All Clear would go soon.

Gordon suddenly dived under the bench and pulled out a large box.

"Wanna sweet?"

Jennifer stared, mesmerised, at the brightly coloured sweets winking up at her. Sherbet dabs, barley-sugar twists, Fry's Chocolate Cream bars, a slab of toffee, a bar of plain chocolate . . . sweets galore! Cain must be bringing her ration home and the two of them were sharing the goodies!

She felt angry but too frightened to say anything. Cain, bent over his wireless, never even looked up.

"No, thank you," she said primly.

The cellar door opened and Gordon quickly shoved the box back under the bench as Mrs Draper came down the stone steps with a tray of lemonade and broken biscuits.

"OK, kids?" she asked. "The All Clear won't be long, Jennifer, then you can look for your Humphrey."

Mrs Draper beamed at them all, pulled a ball of green wool and two needles out of her overall pocket, sat down and started knitting. Cain looked up.

"Is Humphrey your funny black cat with the mangled ear?"

"Yes, he was in a fight," Jennifer said. "Now he's run away."

"Silly name for a cat!" Gordon said.

"It's Humphrey Bogart, really. Mum's got a crush on that film star bloke," Jennifer gabbled.

The boys burst out laughing. Jennifer began to cry. She couldn't help it.

"Girls — ugh!" Gordon exclaimed.

"Shut up, Gordon!" Cain yelled suddenly.

"Boys!" Mrs Draper snapped. "Bring your lemonade over here and sit with me, Jennifer," she added, smiling.

FOR what seemed like hours, Jennifer sat listening to Mrs Draper's clicking needles and the boys bickering. Then, thankfully, the All Clear sounded.

She felt better. That first siren, with its long, sinister wail, always made her shiver, but the All Clear was different. She stood up to go, but Cain beat her to it.

"I'm off!" he cried.

"Just a minute!" his mother called, dropping her knitting and rushing up the steps after him.

I bet he's off to cadge someone else's sweet coupons, Jennifer thought.

"Your Mr Bogart could be in Casablanca by now!" Gordon laughed, pulling out his box once more. "What shall I have? The last bar of plain chocolate, I think . . . Cain's favourite!"

On her way out of the house Jennifer passed Mrs Draper going back to the cellar.

"Thank you —" Jennifer began, but Mrs Draper interrupted her.

"Dunno where Cain's belted off to, but I might just catch Gordon out.

Little devils, they think I don't know what they've got stashed away in that box! Wait till I get my hands on them!"

Outside in the sunshine, Jennifer decided to go home. Mum would be back by now and Humphrey had been heading that way earlier. Maybe he was already there, mewing for his tea. On the way, she peered into gardens calling his name.

Passing a sweet shop, she looked inside for Cain, but he wasn't there. Fancy Mrs Draper knowing about those sweets! Cain was in for it, good and proper — served him right! Maybe now she'd get to keep her own coupons. Gordon's chocolate bar had looked really yummy . . .

Back home, she crossed her fingers as she went inside. Please let Humphrey be here!

"Ah, there you are, Jennifer!" Mum exclaimed. "You all right?"

"Gran was out. I've been with the Drapers," Jennifer answered. "Humphrey ran away — has he come back?"

"No! I wondered why he hadn't come in for his tea."

Jennifer bit her lip. He was lost for ever. She couldn't bear it!

JENNIFER was brought back to the present by a commotion in front of her. Sean was shouting, his voice clear and loud above the noise in the shop.

"I'm warning you, Dumbo. I'll tell Miss Morris!"

Jennifer took one look at Dumbo's stricken face and decided it was time to act.

"Really?" Her voice was icy.

Sean looked up, startled.

"You take the boy's money and I'll tell Miss Morris about you. OK?"

She stared into Sean's brown eyes. She could be Miss Morris's best friend, for all he knew. Truth was, she didn't even recognise their school uniform. But it did the trick. Sean mumbled something inaudible, tossed his head, then turned and left the shop. Dumbo looked up at her gratefully.

"Thanks, missus."

Jennifer, relieved at the outcome, smiled at him as she shuffled forward in the unruly queue. Nearly at the counter! Her cat, Sprout, would only eat one brand of cat food.

So different from old Humphrey, who'd eat any scraps from their plates. It didn't do for cats — or people, come to that — to be fussy when there was a war on. Amazing how clearly she remembered the day Humphrey Bogart went missing . . .

✳   ✳   ✳   ✳

Jennifer sat in the yellow sitting-room, trying not to cry.

"He'll turn up," Mum said, not very hopefully, her arm around Jennifer.

146

Brixham

SEVEN miles south of Totnes, on Devon's glorious Torbay, lies Brixham, reputedly home to the largest fishery in England back in 1850.

One of the main attractions in the harbour these days is the replica of a world-famous ship. In 1577-80, *The Golden Hind* took Francis Drake around the globe, on so prosperous a voyage that on his return Queen Elizabeth knighted him at Greenwich.

These days the ship is a major tourist attraction — and some people even get married on board!

Also at the harbour is a statue marking Brixham's day in the sun. This is where William of Orange first set foot on arrival in Britain at the start of the Glorious Revolution in 1688. The statue was put up for the bicentenary of the occasion.

The upper part of the town, Higher Brixham, also has an important claim to fame, being the place where Henry Lyte wrote "Abide With Me" while vicar of All Saints.

J. CAMPBELL KERR.

There was a knock on the door.

Two minutes later Cain, of all people, marched in, carrying a fat black cat with a mangled ear. Jennifer gaped as he dumped Humphrey on her lap.

"Found him squatting in a garden, waiting for a bird for his dinner," Cain explained.

Jennifer was choked. Cain Draper, who pinched her sweet coupons, had been out searching for her cat. Why would he do that?

"You're a good lad, Cain!" Mum was all smiles. "Sit down — I'll get you some tea."

Mum went into the kitchen and Jennifer hugged Humphrey.

"Thanks, Cain," was all she could say.

Cain was tracing the square pattern on the lino with the toe of his boot.

"Er . . . about the coupons. Gordon made me do it. He's right greedy for sweets and said he'd belt into me if I didn't get the extra coupons. He took my pocket money, too, to buy 'em with. And when I saw you with Colin — "

"Cain, I don't even like Colin Butts!"

Cain shrugged and Jennifer noticed that the side of his face she could see was a fiery red.

"I s'pose I was jealous . . ."

Jennifer frowned at him. Jealous? Of her and Colin?

Her own face felt very hot as she realised what he was saying. She should answer but she was tongue-tied, as her mother called it. In a minute she would tell Cain that his mum had discovered their little secret. But, for now, she just smiled shyly. Suddenly Cain's big blue eyes and floppy red hair seemed really interesting . . .

DUMBO bought his bag of liquorice, grinned at her and was gone. Jennifer, in turn, purchased Sprout's dinner along with a couple of other items.

She left the shop, swinging her carrier bag, still thinking back. From that day, when Cain Draper said he was jealous, she had begun to see him — and life in general — in an entirely different light. That episode marked the beginning of the process of growing up for her.

Jennifer sang to herself as she walked. Taking into account all the hardships and joys over the years, things had turned out well. Two daughters, three grandsons . . . and of course her lovely husband, waiting at home for her.

Sitting in the bag beside the cat food was a large slab of plain dark chocolate, Cain's favourite.

Jennifer smiled. She and Cain had each gone their separate ways after the war and it was years before they met up again. But they belonged together, no doubt about that.

She'd give him a big hug when she got home. And there would be a special hug for Sprout — in memory of Humphrey Bogart. ∎

waiting in the wings

I SAW it as soon as we all tumbled off the school bus — a new poster on the parish council noticeboard.

"Look!" Grabbing Jo's arm, I pulled her across to it. *"Auditions for a brand-new play by well-known local writer Miranda Green."*

"Well known, my foot," Jo snorted. "Remember 'Aladdin' two years ago? It takes something for a village panto to fold on the first night of a two-night run. Dad said . . ."

by Annie Harris.

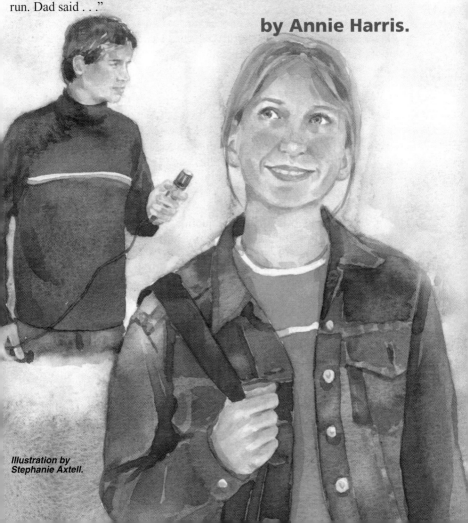

Illustration by Stephanie Axtell.

I wasn't listening to what her dad had said. I'd just seen who the producer was going to be. Oliver Tate. He'd recently come back to live with his mother in one of the new houses at the far end of the village while studying for an MA or something in Performing Arts at the local university.

He was tall, dark and very handsome and he sent shivers up and down my spine whenever I saw him in the distance. And distance was the operative word. Oliver Tate didn't know that I even existed — up until now.

"I'm going to the audition," I said.

"You?" Jo looked at me as if I'd just grown two heads.

"Why not? I'm thinking of going in for acting as a career."

"Since when? Oh, Sam, don't be daft."

"I told you last month, when we went to Stratford. Judi Dench, she was — oh, marvellous."

That evening I'd walked back in a dreamworld to where the school minibus was parked, hardly aware of the rest of my English group fooling around or the cold wind coming off the river. It didn't even bother me any more that we'd had to wear our stupid school uniforms — even the hat. I knew then that acting was what I wanted to do.

"I told you," I repeated.

"Yeah, but I thought you were just joking. Look what happened the last time you acted — it was a disaster."

I gave her a haughty look. There were times when even I could go off my very oldest and dearest friend.

"No, it wasn't."

"It was, Sam." Jo wasn't giving up. "All you had to do was go on on all fours and say 'Baa' a couple of times."

"Well, Gran's sheepskin rug kept slipping. It wasn't my fault I couldn't see!"

I should perhaps point out that the play concerned was a school nativity play and — as you will have gathered — I was a lamb. Lamb-in-chief, in fact, on the first night, at any rate.

"And anyway," I went on, "everybody gets stage fright when they're six."

TRUST Jo to bring that up. Over ten years ago and she still remembered — probably because she'd laughed so much she had to be taken out. When I'd casually asked Mum and Dad what they thought of my performance, Dad had a choking fit, but Mum looked me straight in the eye.

"You were the hit of the evening, my sweet. Our little star."

I scowled at Jo.

"I'm not the only actress in my family, you know. Have I ever told you about my great-aunt Gwendolyn?"

"I think you might have mentioned her once or twice. In the chorus at the end-of-pier show at Great Yarmouth one summer, wasn't she? The back row of the chorus, I seem to remember."

"Yes, well, it just goes to show. I've got acting in my genes."

Even so, I'd never had the urge to tread the boards again — until now. Suddenly, I saw it all . . .

I was in the West End, understudying. They'd just come through to my dressing-room to tell me that Judi had slipped on her way to the stage door. Everyone would tell me that the show had to go on and that it was all down to me. I would have to go out there and save the day.

Electricians outside the theatre would put up my name in yellow lights. The morning papers would say I was an exciting new talent, the new Judi Dench.

"So what will you do for the audition?" Jo asked.

"Do? What do you mean do?"

"You know, you have to perform something."

I had to think fast.

"I'm doing Ophelia's speech."

We were studying "Hamlet" at school and I'd already learned those lines by heart so that was one thing I wouldn't have to worry about. Jo gave me one last look of disbelief and turned to go up the path to her house.

I WAS the last to be called. When I finally walked out on to the village hall's rickety stage, clutching a bunch of herbs I'd just picked from our garden, I peered out past the lights and saw Oliver. He was wearing a white shirt and cravat and, snuggled up very close to him, was Miranda Green.

Oliver consulted a clipboard.

"Samantha Jones?"

"Y-yes." Fluttering butterflies seemed to have snatched my voice away. I cleared my throat. "Yes."

"And what are you doing for us?"

"The Ophelia speech from 'Hamlet'," I stuttered.

"'Hamlet'? Oh, let's have it, then." He didn't sound very keen, but I wasn't going to let that put me off.

I sorted out a sprig of rosemary and began.

"There's rosemary, that's for remembrance —"

"That isn't rosemary — it's fennel," Miranda's voice called from out of the darkness, and I definitely heard what sounded like a snigger.

"Oh, sorry." I fumbled for another sprig and started again. *"There's rosemary, that's for remembrance. Pray, love, remember. And there —"*

"Right, that's fine." Oliver got briskly to his feet and I saw him glance at his watch. "Thank you, er, Samantha. We'll let you know."

And that was it. As I went out of the back door, still clutching my pathetic bundle of herbs, Oliver and Miranda roared off in the direction of the White Lion in his red MG Midget.

"Hi, Sam."

I turned and saw Andrew Blythe, a boy from my class.

"Hello, Andy. Have you been auditioning?"

"Good grief, no." He gave a snort of laughter. "I'm no actor, unlike you."

"Oh, very funny." I was feeling quite down.

"No, no, I mean it. I was backstage. I'm helping with the scene painting and I saw you. Only from the side, mind, but you were very good."

"Well, thanks, Andy."

It was nice of him to say so, but I knew he was only being kind.

"Do you fancy a lemonade in the White Lion garden?" he went on.

"No, thanks. I've got an English essay to finish, and some French course work."

He pulled a face.

"Poor you. At least with maths and physics I don't get endless essays. Anyway, good luck. I'm sure you'll get a starring role."

WELL, I did get a role — the maid. I was over the moon — until I got my copy of Miranda's masterpiece. Honestly, I swear she'd just cobbled the plot together from half a dozen Agatha Christies. I was — still am — a Christie fan, and I just knew that bits of that play came from two of my favourite books.

I also discovered that as Emily, the maid, I had one line and then I was to be found dead on the carpet at the end of Act One. The murderer would arrive to see the heroine — Miranda, what a surprise — and when I let him in he would recognise me from way back, and because I knew something bad about him which he was afraid I would tell, I was strangled with my frilly cap.

Really, it was awful, but I thought if I turned the part down it would look like sour grapes. I decided what I had to do was put absolutely everything into my one line — *"There's a gentleman to see you, madam."* At least it would be useful experience for me on my way to stardom.

Some things are best told briefly. It's difficult to forget one line, but I managed it on the first night. On the second night I tripped over in Mum's high heels and ended up spreadeagled on the carpet before the murderer could get near me.

And on the last night — it wasn't my fault, whatever Miranda said next day — someone had decided that the artificial flowers on the side table looked a bit dusty and replaced them with a bunch of real chrysanthemums.

As I lay on the carpet at the back of the stage, waiting to be discovered, my nose started itching. Those stupid flowers. My hay fever. I groaned silently, twitched my nose and bit my lip until my eyes watered.

Miranda "found" me, shrieked and ran off stage, shouting.

"Help, someone. Emily has been MURDERED. Arghh!"

And just then, before the lights went out and the curtain came down, I let out a terrific sneeze. And, once I'd started, I couldn't stop.

Sheila's Song

SING a song of sunbeams, shining from above,
  On all my family and friends, everyone I love.
Sing a song of happiness, for this day will be
One of the best that ever was — especially for me!

For I am nearly six years old, yet I have never been
A flower-girl in all my life, till darling Auntie Jean
Asked me to be her bridesmaid, on this, her greatest day,
And now you see me all dressed up, in a fairy tale array.

My dress is sprigged with little flowers, I've flowers in
my hair,
I feel just like a wee princess, as I the glory share,
For I can hear folk whispering . . . they're saying
Auntie Jean
Is just about the bonniest bride that they have ever seen.

And one day, when I'm
  very old, a granny
  in a shawl,
I will remember
  Auntie Jean,
  my favourite
  aunt of all,
And how she
  married
  Hamish,
  when the
  sun burst
  from the
  sky,
With her little
  flower-girl —
  that's me —
  called Sheila,
  standing by!
— Kathleen
O'Farrell.

As I fled, I could still hear the audience roaring and stamping their feet. I didn't go backstage, where on the other two nights I'd waited to do my curtain call. Instead I ran straight out into the deserted carpark.

I was standing there, blowing my nose and mopping my streaming eyes, when Andy appeared.

"Oh, Sam, you were brilliant." He was still laughing, but I was too mortified to care.

"No, I wasn't," I wailed. "I've ruined the whole thing."

"Rubbish. You saved the night."

"But Oliver and Miranda will never forgive me."

"So? Who cares about that pair of creeps?"

Yes, who did care? Close up, Oliver's eyes were very close together, and his smile was crooked. And anyway,

The "Friend" Remembers Wartim Chanteuses & Entertainers
Betty Driver MBE b 1920

MANY of you will know this lady as Betty Turpin of "Coronation Street" fame!

Born in Leicester, Betty Driver moved to Manchester when she was two years old. She has been in showbusiness since the age of nine, starting at the Terance Byron Rep in Manchester.

She has made many appearances on radio, in West End plays and revues, films and world tours with her own show.

From 1941 she spent seven years as featured artist with the internationally famous dance bandleader, Henry Hall.

During World War II she travelled with the band, entertaining the troops, and visited France, Germany and Holland with her act.

These days, Betty can regularly be seen on TV, pulling pints at the Rover's Return in her role as Betty Turpin in the popular soap "Coronation Street". It had long been an ambition of hers to appear on the programme, which she joined back in 1969.

since I'd seen him nuzzling Miranda's neck in the wings while she stood there looking even dopier than usual — well, I do have standards.

"So you're not going to the party?"

"Definitely not."

"In that case we'll have a party on our own. In the White Lion garden. And I promise you, Sammy — you'll laugh about all this one day."

AND I do laugh about it as I get ready. It's our wedding anniversary and we're going to the theatre, my husband and I. I still get a kick from saying that, even after twenty-four years. Andy has lovely eyes and at least they're not close together, like some people's.

He smiles at me now as he arrives home from work and dumps his briefcase.

154

Betty Driver

Betty has travelled the length and breadth of the country and has appeared at just about every major variety theatre in the country. She was awarded the MBE in 2000.

"School OK?"

"Yes, fine, although I think we'll all be glad when term ends."

You will not be too surprised to hear that Judi — Dame Judi now, of course — still reigns supreme, while I've been a teacher of English and Drama for over twenty years. Somehow, I've turned out to be a better teacher of Drama than actress, although still, at the end of almost every term, a class will ask me to "Do your Ophelia bit, miss. Please!"

So, to oblige my punters, I kick off my shoes and launch into *"There's rosemary . . ."*

We live quite near Stratford now, so we go to the theatre as often as we can. But tonight is special. Dame Judi is back, her performance a triumph. We're in the stalls — usually we're quite a bit further away but, as I said, tonight is special and I don't want to miss anything.

As we walk from the carpark, the chill wind is still coming off the river, still tinkling the strings of coloured lights. Inside the theatre, there's a hum of anticipation. The exit doors close softly, the lights go down and then she's there, and I can't see anyone else.

She looks very demure, as a young servant girl should. And now I can't see anything at all, for the tears in my eyes. I turn my head and look at Andy, who pulls a funny little face and squeezes my hand for a moment, before we look back at the stage, where our daughter, Kristina, is just curtseying (perfectly) to her mistress, Dame Judi.

They're funny things, genes. I didn't have the acting one, after all — but somehow I passed it on. And, an even funnier thing, I'm much prouder of Kristina than I would have been of myself. ■

I KNOW you want to go." Matthew sighed. "But I can't take you."

"It's a special day for me." Matthew's grandfather looked hopeful. "And I'd love to share it with my only grandson."

"Gramps!" Matthew held up his hands. "Don't try to make me feel worse than I do already."

"Your mum usually goes to the Remembrance Service with me," Joe continued, undeterred. "And it's only for an hour or so on Sunday morning."

"Dad's taken her to visit a friend who's ill. And she certainly didn't say anything to me about Sunday."

GRANDPA JOE'S MEMORY BOX

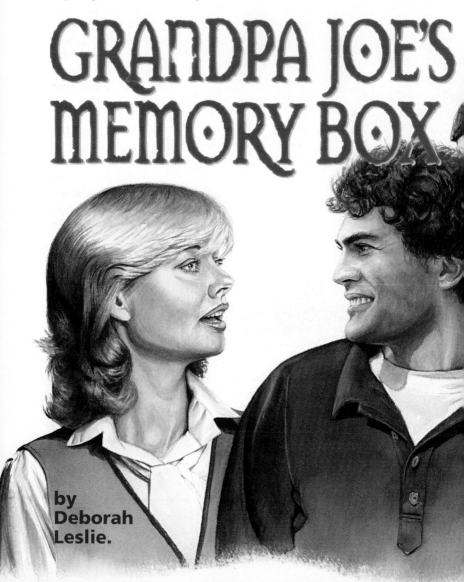

by
Deborah
Leslie.

"I know all about that," Joe said, shaking his head impatiently. "And she wouldn't have mentioned it, because she sorted everything out before she left. The hospital transport was going to take me." He sighed and looked irritated.

"We thought we had it all arranged, but it looks like there's a problem — something to do with the driver and insurance — more rules and regulations."

"I'm really sorry about that, Grandpa, but I just can't manage." Matthew felt a warm flush creep up over his neck and face.

Illustration by Shane Marsh.

"You don't even have to come to the church, if you don't want to," Joe said, lowering his expectations. "You could just drop us off."

"Us?"

"Yes, us. Me and William, of course."

"Your ears must have been burning," Matthew said, looking up as William shuffled into the hospital ward, his slippers making a soft scuffing sound against the polished floor. Matthew smiled warmly at his grandfather's friend. William was much quieter than Joe, a real gentle giant of a man.

"I was just telling Matthew about our transport problems for Sunday." Joe turned to face his friend as William sat down heavily in an armchair.

"Rules and regulations," William said, shaking his head. He fell silent for a moment. "We served in the same regiment, you know. And we always go to the service together."

"Wouldn't miss it," Joe added. "I'm laying the poppy wreath at the memorial."

"It makes no difference. Grandpa, I still can't take you. It's my weekend off and I've got something planned."

"By your face, I'm guessing it's a woman, then."

157

Matthew nodded.

"Well, I suppose that's more important than taking your old grandfather to the Remembrance Day service," Joe said, the disappointment evident in his eyes.

"Her name's Susan. And we're going to see her parents in Glasgow. We're both staying over for the weekend — I can't let her down." Matthew looked uncomfortable.

AH, well," Joe said, a smile lighting up his lined features, "that's different. It's about time you were thinking of getting married."

"I'm not getting married, Grandpa," Matthew protested. "It's only a visit."

"I've been around a good deal longer than you, lad." Joe's blue eyes crinkled at the corners and twinkled with mischief. "And when a girl wants to take you home to meet her parents. . . "

"Just drop it, Gramps."

"Leave the lad alone, Joe." William gave a low chuckle.

"How's the waiting list for the retirement home going?" Matthew asked, anxious to change the subject.

"We're getting nearer the top." Joe fumbled in his locker, pulled out a bag of mints and handed them round. "But wherever we go, we want to go together, eh, William?"

William nodded.

"You're a right pair," Matthew said, sucking on his sweet and laughing. "Joined at the hip."

"Arthritic hips at that," William put in, giving a slow smile.

"You're a real double act." Matthew looked at the two old friends. "It seems somehow fitting that you should end up in here at the same time."

"Did you know the house is up for sale?" Joe asked, the laughter suddenly dying on his lips. "It's going to be hard to let it go."

"It's a family house with stairs and a big garden, Gramps — too big for you on your own. And you're always saying that you get lonely in the evenings now that Grandma's not here."

"I've got some stuff in the attic for the charity shop," Joe said, ignoring his grandson's reasoning. "Your dad sorted it out for me. It's all packed into a big red plastic box. You'll easily see it."

"But I haven't got time to do that today."

"It wouldn't take you a minute," Joe insisted, already searching in his bedside locker for his house keys. "Anyway, your mother wants to make a start on packing everything up when she comes back."

"Anything else?" Matthew smiled good-humouredly. "Before you organise the rest of my life for me."

"Actually, yes," Joe said, already getting up from his chair. "I'd quite like to be introduced to this Susan. If you're going to meet her family, I think it's only fair that she should meet yours. And what better place to start than with your old grandfather?"

"OK, Grandpa." Matthew was laughing now as he smiled at the old man who'd been an important part of his life for as long as he could remember. "You win. I'll nip round to your place, pick up the box, and ask Susan if she'd like to meet you."

"YOU'RE late!" Susan was standing tapping her watch as Matthew came charging around the corner, red faced and gasping for breath.

"I'm sorry, love. I went to visit my grandpa at the hospital. Big mistake," he added with a smile. "I hope you don't mind —" he looked apologetic "— but he wants me to go to his house and pick up a box of junk for the charity shop."

"Oh, you are a sweetie, aren't you?" Susan smiled, his tardiness forgiven. "You always have time for other people — just one of the things I love about you."

Matthew flushed at her compliment, half with pleasure and half with guilt as he remembered the Sunday service.

"What is it?" Susan asked, seeming to sense his discomfort.

"Grandpa did say he wanted to meet you," he said quickly, unwilling to let her in on the real reason for his preoccupation.

"Well, that's nothing to worry about. I'd love to!"

"Really?"

"Of course," she said, catching his hand as they walked. "Tell you what, why don't we skip the coffee? We'll go back to the car, pick up the box from your grandpa's, then pop in by the hospital and I can say a quick hello. And that leaves us free to head off at the time we'd planned."

∗   ∗   ∗   ∗

Matthew turned the key and pushed open the door of his grandfather's house. The lingering smell of pipe tobacco wafted up to meet him as he stepped over the pile of junk mail.

"Come on in," he said as Susan followed him inside.

"Where's the box for the charity shop?" Susan closed the front door and picked up the brightly coloured leaflets from the mat.

"In the attic." Matthew was already climbing the stairs. "Will you check the downstairs rooms and have a look out the back to make sure everything's OK?"

Upstairs, he moved quickly from room to room before pulling down the ladder that led to the attic.

The metal rungs creaked beneath his weight as he climbed.

He flicked on a dusty light switch, sniffing at the damp smell and looking around at the piles of junk and cobwebs that hung from the rafters. Despite the clutter, he felt a warm glow wash over him. As a child, the attic had always held a great fascination — that special place where Grandpa Joe had taken him to play.

Matthew smiled as his eyes became accustomed to the gloom and finally found their prize: the train track, complete with engines, signposts and signal box.

He dropped to his knees beside the track, closing his eyes as he remembered.

DON'T tell your gran I've been smoking up here, Matthew. Apparently it's a fire hazard, what with all this stuff that's lying around."

"Let's both eat one of your mints, Gramps," Matthew suggested, already holding out his hand. "Then maybe she won't be able to smell the tobacco."

"Good idea, lad." Joe grinned and produced two sweets from the pocket of his cardigan.

"What's in that box?" Matthew asked, pointing to an old wooden trunk set away from the train track and leaning towers of cardboard boxes.

"Ah, well, that's my special chest for all my treasures." Joe gave a secretive smile. "It's my memory box."

"I thought you kept all your memories in here." Matthew crunched noisily on the mint and tapped a finger against his forehead.

"That's right, son, I do. But the things I keep in the chest help me to remember — to make sure I never forget."

"Can I see?" Matthew moved to stand beside the box and ran both chubby hands over the worn wood.

"When you're old enough to understand, I'll let you see inside," Joe promised.

"But, Grandpa, I'm big now. I'm grown up . . ." Matthew's voice tailed away.

"You're a good boy, Matthew." Joe patted him on the head. "And there's plenty of time for you to be a man."

"How will I know when it's time, Gramps?"

"You'll just know," Joe said, pulling him into the warmth of his embrace.

Matthew snuggled against the softness of his grandfather's cardigan, breathing in the comforting aroma of old wool, pipe tobacco and mints. He sighed happily, the memory box already forgotten.

*　　*　　*　　*

Matthew was startled from his reverie by the sound of footsteps on the metal ladder.

"Can't you find it?" Susan asked, her face, framed in a shiny black bob,

Glencoe

ONE of Scotland's most famous glens, Glencoe's rugged attraction draws flocks of tourists to gaze in awe at its peaks and shadowy, scree-filled ravines.

When the mists curl down from the mountains and close in on the narrow glen, it can be a forbidding place, but whatever the season, there's no denying its breathtaking, dramatic beauty.

J. CAMPBELL KERR.

appearing above the trap door.

"It's over there, just by the hatch." Matthew scrambled to his feet and nodded at the big red plastic box full of cups and saucers, odd rolls of wallpaper and old paperback books. "I was just having a look around — and remembering," he added, jerking a thumb at the cobweb-covered railway line before brushing the dust from the knees of his jeans.

"Boys and their toys, eh?" Susan smiled as she pulled herself up through the trap door. "I thought you'd got lost."

"Did you have a good look around downstairs?" Matthew grabbed her hands and helped her up.

"Everything's fine." She gave a little sigh. "It's such a lovely family house. I could really see myself living somewhere like this. It's got so much character."

"I know what you mean. I've always loved it here. When I was a boy I'd spend most of the summer holidays with Granny and Grandpa."

AND then it seemed as if time stood still as Matthew stared, entranced, at Susan as she continued to enthuse about the house and garden, her dark eyes dancing under a silky-smooth fringe. And, in that moment, he knew that he loved her.

"Are you ready, then?" she asked, breaking the spell.

"Just a minute." Matthew crossed the wooden floorboards and found what he was looking for.

"What's this?" Susan moved to stand at his side as he stood looking down at his grandfather's old wooden chest.

"It's Grandpa Joe's memory box. He always promised to let me see inside when I was old enough. Do you think I'm old enough now?" He smiled, feeling like a little boy again as he posed the question.

"Do you think you should?" Susan bit her bottom lip. "Isn't this kind of private stuff?"

"I just want to take a quick look. Gramps won't ever know." He turned the key and pulled open the lid.

Matthew felt a wave of disappointment wash over him as he stared down into the depths of the chest. Where were the treasures his childish imagination had pictured?

The trunk was full of photographs, faded newspaper cuttings, old wedding invitations, and home-made Christmas, birthday and Father's Day cards.

"I don't know what I thought would be in here," Matthew said, reading a Christmas card he'd made at primary school. "I guess I always thought it would be something more exciting. Hang on a minute, though. What have we got here?"

Matthew reached down into the chest and lifted out a tatty old shoebox. The box was secured with a yellowing elastic band and smelled like old books. He coughed and sneezed as he blew a furry layer of dust from its lid.

"Look at this, Susan." He lifted the lid and gently pushed aside the red paper poppies that covered the commemorative orders of service from the recent VE and VJ celebrations. Underneath was a bundle of black and white photographs of his grandfather and comrades during the war.

I THINK that's Grandpa," he said, holding one up and pointing to a uniformed figure in the back row. "And I think that's his pal, William, standing next to him."

"Look what's in here," Susan said, opening a worn leather pouch and holding up four wartime medals. The watery sunshine from the skylight brightened the coloured ribbons and caught the glint of metal as they swung from her hand. "I wonder what they're for."

"I don't know . . ." Matthew felt quite ashamed, and he pulled a pile of handwritten letters and a leather-bound diary from the box.

For the next two hours they sat in silence, reading from the faded ink, before Susan finally spoke.

"Did you know your grandfather was one of the first soldiers to go ashore during the D-Day Landings?"

"He's told me the story plenty of times." Matthew lifted his head to meet her gaze. "But I've never appreciated how it really was until I read the entry in his diary. But what he didn't tell me was that his pal William saved his life that day — he actually risked his own life to save Gramps."

"A friend indeed."

Matthew nodded, looking down at an old photograph of the two comrades with their arms around each other's shoulders. He suddenly acknowledged the strength of their friendship and the sorrow and laughter they'd shared.

"What's wrong?" Susan put a consoling hand on his shoulder.

"I knew all about Grandpa's early life, but I only ever listened with half an ear. The truth is, I've never really understood what he's been through — he was so young and so afraid."

"Don't be so hard on yourself. You're the most thoughtful man I've ever met. And I, for one, am proud to know you."

Matthew was suddenly lost for words as he looked up.

"And do you think you could be proud to be my wife?" he said, finally finding his voice.

"Oh, Matthew! If that's a proposal, there's nothing I'd like more!"

Matthew's heart was full and his hands were shaking as they knelt together on the wooden floorboards and carefully repacked Grandpa Joe's memory box before returning it to its resting place.

"You took your time," Joe said, smiling over his grandson's shoulder at Matthew's pretty young companion. "I thought you were driving down to Glasgow tonight."

"I . . . we got held up at the house. And it looks like you might have found yourself a buyer." Matthew turned and gave Susan a conspiratorial wink.

"It's someone you know — someone who mightn't object to you dropping by for the odd visit."

"Who's that, then?"

"I'll tell you all about it later, Gramps. After you and William have met my fiancée, Susan," he said, giving his grandfather a look that warned him not to ask too much.

IANCÉE, eh?" Joe looked taken aback by his grandson's exciting news. He cleared his throat and smiled, before extending a tremulous hand to the pretty young girl.

"I'm very pleased to meet you, lass."

"Likewise." William nodded and smiled.

"I just wanted to say a quick hello before the Remembrance Service," Susan said, sitting down on the edge of Joe's bed.

"But aren't you two supposed to be going away for the weekend?"

"Not any more. We've changed our plans," Matthew said, placing a small leather pouch in his grandfather's hand. "I thought you might need these for Sunday."

"Ah!" Joe's face lit up at the sight of his treasured war medals. "Looks like someone's been through my memory box."

"I hope you don't mind, Gramps."

"Not at all, lad. After all, I did promise that when you were old enough to understand, you'd see what was inside. I wanted you to know what's important in life — the things I hold dear. And I wanted you to know about the proud young men who fought for their country, to give you the freedom you enjoy today."

Matthew swallowed a lump in his throat as he looked from his grandfather to William, a new and previously undiscovered pride for the two old soldiers rising in his chest; the words he'd heard a hundred times suddenly taking on a new and deeper meaning.

"You made a good decision today, son," Joe said, struggling to his feet. "I'm proud of you."

"And I'm proud of you, Gramps — and of William, and every other brave soldier. And I'll be proud to wear my poppy on Sunday and even prouder when I watch you lay the wreath at the memorial."

Matthew held his grandfather's gaze.

"Do you think that means I'm old enough now — old enough to understand?"

Joe nodded, a solitary tear running down his cheek.

"You've always been a good boy, Matthew — and now it's time to be a man." ■

The Mistletoe Bough

by Pamela Kavanagh.

Illustration by Lesley Ann Mackenzie.

WOMEN?" Jacob Firkettle pursed his lips reflectively. "They're all right in their place, I reckon — cooking and cleaning, and what have you. But show me the one who can tackle the sort of day we put in! 'Tisn't credible.

"And another thing, they will try and boss you. Do this, do that, never a moment to call your own. You're better off stopping single like me, boy. You can please yourself then."

Speech over, Jacob cut himself a wedge of hard red cheese and turned his attention to supper, while Luke stared silently at his cooling mug of tea.

Ever since coming to lodge with Jacob in his tied cottage, Luke had taken the ploughman's advice. Jacob might not be able to read or write, but he carried a store of knowledge in his head.

If you needed to know how to thatch a roof or layer a hedge, then Jacob was your man. As for ploughing — nobody ploughed a straighter furrow, and that was what Luke was here to learn.

So great was his progress that the master had raised his position to under-ploughman here at Stacks Farm, with all it entailed, and there was the nub.

With an increase in wage and the chance of a cottage, Luke would be in a position to wed.

Over the meal he had mentioned the fact, but when it came to matters of the heart, Jacob was not quite so forthcoming.

"Who is this girl that's taken your fancy, anyway?" the ploughman enquired.

"Verity Bates." The very mention of her name brought a tightness to Luke's throat.

Verity's trim form and pert smile had captured his attention one morning when he had gone to the dairy for milk.

That had been around harvest time. It was winter now, the corn and barley long in, but his feelings had not changed.

"The dairymaid?" Jacob munched his bread and cheese. "She's a bonnie wench, I'll say that much. Puts me in mind of Betty at the same age."

A softening in his tone made Luke glance up.

"Oh?"

"Set her cap at me years ago, did Betty Sarne. She was kitchenmaid then, but she's worked her way up to cook.

"Wouldn't have been cook if I'd put a ring on her finger, would she? Queen of the roost, all those girls to boss? I reckon I did Betty a favour by not wedding her."

"Weren't you feared she'd find someone else?"

"Not Betty. 'Twas me she wanted, and that's a fact. I expect young Verity's the same over yourself."

"Not exactly." Luke pushed away his untouched supper. "Verity goes out of her way to avoid me. Goodness knows why."

"Ah. Happen she needs some encouragement. When I was a lad, a fellow wore a sprig of honeysuckle in his cap when he was sweet on a girl. Worked like a charm, it did."

"Where would I find honeysuckle in December?" Luke said scathingly.

"Mistletoe, then. You get a kiss for every berry on the twig.

"Nothing wrong in a bit of fun, boy. Just watch you don't get bamboozled into putting that ring on her finger, that's all." Jacob paused, his eyes glinting merrily.

"There's mistletoe growing in the orchard around now, and those girls take a short cut through there to the dairy. All you need to do is bide your chance."

＊　　＊　　＊　　＊

He was there at first light, catching his breath nervously as Verity came tripping over the frosted grass towards him, her shawl clutched about her against the chill winter dawn.

"'Morning, Verity."

"Why, Luke, good morning. Was it the milk you wanted? You're too early. We've not skimmed it yet."

"'Twasn't that." His gaze slid to the sprays of mistletoe on the apple bough, and Verity tossed her head.

"Kisses, is it? See me falling for that old ruse, Luke Renfrew! Out of my way. Some of us have work to do!"

She went hurrying off, laughter tinkling in her wake. Luke, rather red in the face, made his way to the stables and the great grey plough-horses, who were, he thought ruefully, a great deal easier to manage than girls.

He groomed his team until the bite had gone out of the ground, then harnessed them up and drove them to the five-acre, which was already three-quarters turned.

Eyeing his furrows critically, seeing that every one ran straight and true in line with the thorn hedge, Luke was satisfied. With luck he should get the field done by nightfall.

He hitched up the coulter and clicked his tongue to the horses, who heaved their weight into their collars and went plodding obediently off.

Luke's problems were forgotten as he bent his back to the work, a cloud of gulls crying after him along the ridges of new-turned earth.

As he laboured he sang, his true tenor voice ringing out across the slopes.

So early in the morning the plough-boy went his way
All hastening to the stables for to begin his day . . .

In the dairy, Verity looked up. That would be Luke on the five-acre. Old Jacob had a voice fit to curdle the cream, but Luke, now . . . Luke could charm the birds from their nests with his singing.

Smiling a little wistfully, she began to churn the butter.

ON the lower slopes, Jacob was tilling with his three-horse team. He, too, heard Luke's singing, and glanced up towards the tall youth behind the plough, bare-headed as always.

A voice shouting his name caught his attention. Standing by the gate was a womanly figure in a blue cloak, a basket covered by a checked cloth in her hand.

Betty with the midday meal! Jacob's mouth watered. With luck, it would be meat and vegetable pasties — his favourite, and none so good as Betty's.

He saw to the horses, and made his way down the field to where she waited.

"I've put in a crock of tea." Betty handed him the basket of food. "Mind you drink it before it cools. There's pasties, too."

He nodded his thanks, the tantalising smell of crusty pastry and onions in his nostrils.

"Only another five days till Christmas. Are the master and mistress expecting company this year?" he asked conversationally.

"Just the boys, as usual." Now grown men with families of their own, to Betty the two Stacks youngsters would always be known as the boys. "And the wives and children, of course. I expect we'll see you at the Christmas Eve supper?"

"Aye, no doubt." Stacks Farm on Christmas Eve was by tradition an open house, with all the staff welcome, and Jacob looked forward to the event.

"There's some won't be able to spend Christmas with their folks," Betty went on, "Verity for one. Her people live too far away. It's a goodly walk and you can't rely on the weather at this time of year."

"That's true." Jacob sniffed the wind. "Be snowing before morning, I don't doubt."

"Then you'd better get on with this field." Betty smiled, dimples appearing briefly in her firm country cheeks. "Mind you bring that crock back with you, and not leave it for the horses to trample like last time. 'Bye, Jacob. Enjoy your lunch."

Jacob watched her leave and thanked Providence for a close escape. How women nagged! A man was better off without them.

✳   ✳   ✳   ✳

At my age, I should know better, Betty admonished herself as she headed back to the house. Getting up early simply to bake for someone who doesn't appreciate what's been done, and never will! But there, concocting sundry treats for Jacob was force of habit, and Betty knew she would go on making his meat pasties and gingerbread till her last breath was drawn.

She gained the farmyard, where the hens came flocking up in the hope of grain. Shooing them away crossly, Betty entered the kitchen to start her preparations for Christmas.

She was lining up crocks of mincemeat when Verity appeared with the milk.

"If you've got a moment to spare, Betty, I wanted a word with you about Luke," the girl said hesitantly, placing the jugs on the table. "I've done as you suggested and not appeared too keen, but 'tisn't working. Luke backs off and I don't see any more of him for ages."

"Maybe he's playing the same game, and I've a good idea who's put him up to it. That Jacob drove me to distraction with his tricks! Pretending not to have noticed when I wore a new bonnet, sending me Valentines and then swearing he knew nothing about it. And I knew all the time he liked me — a lot."

"Weren't you tempted to go out with someone else?" Verity asked. "Make him jealous? It worked with Rose's Sam. She danced with everyone bar him at the Plough Monday celebrations, and by Eastertide they were wed."

"Jacob was too canny for that. He'd have given me his blessing and gone off laughing!"

"But would he have meant it?"

"Perhaps. It could be that Jacob's not the marrying kind. Can't speak for your Luke, of course."

"He's not my Luke," Verity said in a small voice. She looked so downcast that Betty felt a pang. Maybe this romance needed a different sort of helping hand?

She'd have to keep her eyes skinned. Some way was bound to show itself.

The Wedding Breakfast

*T*HE family home is
   ringing now, with joyful,
chattering folk,
And this small room is
   crowded, to its full capacity,
As Father tells his one and
   only, well-remembered joke,
And dainty food is handed
   round by smiling
   Jess McPhee.

"Everything has
   gone so well,"
   says Mother
   (though in
   truth,
Her smart new
   shoes are
   pinching her . . .
   she's rather
   weary, too),
And everyone
   agrees with her, while jolly Auntie Ruth
Admits, "I cried when I saw the bride — but then,
   I always do!"

And many another might confess they've shed a happy tear,
For they have known our Jeanie since she was a tiny girl,
Dancing up and down the street, as though with wings upon
   her feet,
And now a lovely, gentle bride, all shimmering like a pearl!

So many people have worked hard, have done their
   level best
To make this a momentous day, a day to stand apart,
And, with their efforts, they have raised it far above the rest,
A shining memory, to live on in everybody's heart.
                                        — *Kathleen O'Farrell.*

Luke bedded down his horses for the night and left the yard. He had seen Jacob talking to Betty Sarne, and thought, with a jolt of surprise, what a likely couple they made.

Tramping on through the gathering gloom, snowflakes beginning to fall softly, Luke had to wonder how genuine was Jacob's waffling about the merits of the bachelor life, and how much had become habit. They'd looked friendly enough to him.

INDOORS at last, Luke set about lighting the fire and swung the kettle over it for tea.

For the first time it occurred to him how sparse the cottage was. No rag rug by the hearth, no curtains at the window or dainty plates on the dresser shelf . . . no woman's touch.

He pictured coming home to Verity, the firelight burnishing her brown hair, maybe a babe in her arms, their house neat and welcoming, and shook his head hopelessly. Verity had made it all too clear what she thought of him. What was the point in dreaming?

He glanced at the mantel clock. Jacob was late.

Given that the ploughman had three horses to stable when he got back, Luke supposed he'd better get on with the supper. He set the table and put the pan of broth to simmer, between trips outside to peer through the snowy night.

The suppertime broth was cooking fragrantly by the time a stamping of snow-crusted boots on the step announced the return of the householder. Seconds later the door opened. Jacob hung his cap on the peg, shook the snowflakes from his hair and whiskers and strode to the fire to warm his chilled hands.

"You're late," Luke remarked. "Thought you'd got lost."

Jacob looked faintly abashed.

"Truth is, I'd stabled the horses when I remembered leaving something on the slopes and slipped back for it. Took me longer than I'd thought. The snow's settling up there. This puts an end to the ploughing for now."

"Aye. What was it you forgot? Not the tiller?"

"No, it wasn't that. Good of you to bed down the horses for me."

"What? But I didn't. I saw to my two and came straight on here."

"Well, someone must have." Jacob scratched his head in puzzlement. "All groomed and munching their hay, they were, when I got back, content as you please. One of the lads must have seen to them.

"That broth smells good. Let's eat, boy, before it boils away."

The mystery of the unknown ostler preyed on Luke's mind. Next morning he asked the lad who did the odd jobs if he knew who was responsible for rubbing down the three horses and filling up their hayracks, and the lad nodded.

"I noticed Cook going past with her arms full of hay. I asked her if she

170

wanted some help — well, that's heavy work for a female, and she's no spring chicken. As good as snapped my head off, she did. Told me to mind my own business."

"Cook?" Luke stared at him blankly. "But why would Betty Sarne be tending the horses?"

"Search me. Happen she thought to give Jacob a hand. It was snowing heavens hard, and he'd gone back up the track — I thought he'd forgotten to shut the gates, but he came back with the wicker basket Cook delivers the field lunches in, and left it on the kitchen step.

"Why do you want to know?"

"Never you mind," Luke said.

The snow rendered outside chores impossible, so the two men spent the day in the barn, oiling the harness and cleaning the metalwork.

Luke spoke without looking up from the set he was buffing.

"It seems to me you got it wrong about the ladies, Jacob."

"What do you mean?" Jacob asked.

"I made a point of finding out who the good fairy was who saw to the horses for you last night. It was Betty. Made a good job of it, too, you said — for a woman, of course."

Jacob mumbled something incomprehensible into his beard.

"You wouldn't have been avoiding Betty's wrath by doubling back to the fields for that lunch basket of hers?" Luke continued. "Afraid of what she might say, like?"

"I ain't afraid of any woman," Jacob growled. "You know what a fuss they make over their kitchen bits and bobs. Glower on 'em like they've swallowed a wasp! Wasn't worth risking."

"No?" Luke put down the harness and turned the full force of his gaze on the ploughman. "I've got my doubts about that mistletoe charm you put me up to as well. You were having me on."

"Not I! It's a time-honoured way of claiming your sweetheart."

"It made me look a fool. Verity will never take me seriously now."

"'Course she will, boy. Wait till the Christmas Eve supper. You can ask her to dance."

"Some good that will be." Luke looked glum. "When it comes to dancing I've got two left feet."

"Recite a ditty, then, or tell 'em a yarn. Make it about true love, and be sure she knows who you're meaning."

"I couldn't. I'm not poet, nor yet a storyteller."

"Then you've no choice but to give 'em a song. Sure as eggs is eggs, every man and maid there will have to do a turn. It's expected, boy."

Luke cast the ploughman a look that spoke volumes, and reached for a pair of blinkers. The work continued in uneasy silence.

Jacob was far from happy. An uncomfortable atmosphere prevailed in the cottage. Above all he valued Luke's friendship, and he knew he had done the lad no favours. He wanted to make amends.

Not an imaginative man, but possessed of a firm belief in old country lore, Jacob racked his brains and remembered something his grandfather had made every year.

The mistletoe bough, the kissing-bough, a globe of evergreens looped with ribbons and decked with fir cones, shining red apples and sprigs of mistletoe, was hung from a beam where it would revolve slowly in the candle draught. Any young couple who stood beneath it were said to be smiled upon by fortune.

It didn't take long to collect the necessary items, and once the day's work was done, instead of going home, Jacob headed for the garden shed where he had hidden his bounty.

Diligently he set to work, twisting and twining. Later, when all was quiet, he'd sneak into the farmhouse and add the decoration to the others . . .

LAUGHTER and chatter filled the house as master and man gathered together for festivities. A great fire of logs blazed in the massive hearth, garlands of evergreen festooned the walls and baubles twinkled on a tall tree in the corner. Next to it, the mistletoe bough twirled gently in the current of air.

Verity, in rose pink, looked a picture. Luke couldn't keep his eyes off her.

Presiding over a table laden with cold meats, pies, pickles and sweetmeats, Betty in her gown of grey bombazine dished out the fare, adding an extra slice of roast goose to Jacob's already piled platter.

"Many thanks," he said with a conspiratorial wink, his heart quickening at her smile of response.

At the head of the table, the master made his speech, thanking his staff for their loyalty and hard work over the past year and wishing them good health and the compliments of the season. A toast was made, after which the feasting began.

When nothing remained but crumbs, the floor was cleared. Abel Sarkey, the cowman, took up his fiddle, and the dancing began. From his place by the door, Luke watched Verity dipping and whirling to the music. Seeing Jacob claim Betty for a reel, his gaze sharpened.

"Seems I neglected to say how much I appreciated the good turn you did me a few days back," Jacob said, jigging Betty along the aisle of raised arms.

"Don't mention it." Betty was breathless, her cheeks growing fiery — though that could have been exertion and the heat from the fire.

"I made sure and returned your basket of crocks, like you said," Jacob reminded her.

"So you did, Jacob."

The dance drew to a gasping conclusion. Everyone clapped and cheered, and retired to restore their dwindled energies with pints of cider and ginger ale.

"Let's have a recitation. Come on, Sol!" A shout went up, and Sol stood up promptly and launched into "The White Cockade," his party piece and probably the only poem he'd ever learned.

Then Betty's niece, Sarah Jane, began a clog dance, going faster and faster, her quick feet drumming a catchy rhythm on the bare wooden boards of the floor.

"A song next," the master demanded when the girl looked fit to drop, and Jacob, with a wave of his pipe, gestured Luke forward.

Standing directly beneath the mistletoe bough, looking faintly self-conscious, Luke addressed the throng.

"When Jacob told me about having to do a song I wasn't sure what to choose. A carol seemed best, but I daresay we'll all tune up with those later on. Then I remembered a song my mam used to sing. It's from the southern counties where she was born, but likely some of you will know it, so feel free to sing along. Mam called it the Christmas Song."

"But that's what I'm singing!" a voice from the back called out. All eyes turned to see Verity, her face pink and indignant, fists clenched in protest.

"Makes no odds, maid," Jacob smiled at her. "You can sing it together. Be a change to hear a duet. Stand aside, folks, and let her through. That's it."

Verity found herself at Luke's side. Without preamble, he gave her the note and they began, a hush falling as the first phrase of music trilled sweetly to the rafters. When the final notes had died away, there wasn't a dry eye in the place. Jacob cleared his throat noisily and declared the singing the finest he'd ever heard. Luke and Verity were gazing at each other as if nobody else existed.

Afterwards, Jacob never could work out whether it was the mistletoe bough that had worked the magic, or simply chance. But he knew that the image of those two young faces beneath the glimmering twirl of the evergreen globe would be etched for ever in his memory.

He glanced down at Betty. In the flickering firelight her smile was dimpled and youthful. She slipped her arm through his and Jacob, mellowed by good fare and genial company, not to mention a sudden overpowering regard for the woman beside him, did not pull away. ■

Printed and Published in Great Britain by D.C. Thomson & Co., Ltd., Dundee, Glasgow and London.

ISBN 1 84535 155 X
EAN 9 781845 351557

Bognor Regis

BOGNOR REGIS, the popular seaside resort on the south coast of England, lies in the lee of Selsey Bill, sheltered by the Isle of Wight and the South Downs. Bad weather tends to track north or south, leaving Bognor dry and sunny. It has more recorded hours of sunshine than anywhere else in Britain.